THE HIGHLANDER'S HIDDEN HEART
A Medieval Romance Novella

Kathryn Le Veque
Part of the Warrior House of Forbes/de Lohr Dynasty series

The Highlander's Hidden Heart
Copyright © 2017 Kathryn Le Veque
Print Edition

All rights reserved. No part of this book may be used or reproduced in any manner whatsoever without written permission, except in the case of brief quotations embodied in critical articles or reviews.

Kathryn Le Veque Novels

Medieval Romance:

The de Russe Legacy:
The White Lord of Wellesbourne
The Dark One: Dark Knight
Beast
Lord of War: Black Angel
The Iron Knight

The de Lohr Dynasty:
While Angels Slept (Lords of East Anglia)
Rise of the Defender
Steelheart
Spectre of the Sword
Archangel
Unending Love
Shadowmoor
Silversword

Great Lords of le Bec:
Great Protector
To the Lady Born (House of de Royans)
Lord of Winter (Lords of de Royans)

Lords of Eire:
The Darkland (Master Knights of Connaught)
Black Sword
Echoes of Ancient Dreams (time travel)

De Wolfe Pack Series:
The Wolfe
Serpent
Scorpion (Saxon Lords of Hage – Also related to The Questing)
The Lion of the North
Walls of Babylon
Dark Destroyer
Nighthawk
Warwolfe
ShadowWolfe

Ancient Kings of Anglecynn:
The Whispering Night
Netherworld

Battle Lords of de Velt:
The Dark Lord
Devil's Dominion

Reign of the House of de Winter:
Lespada
Swords and Shields (also related to The Questing, While Angels Slept)

De Reyne Domination:
Guardian of Darkness
The Fallen One (part of Dragonblade Series)
With Dreams Only of You

Unrelated characters or family groups:
The Gorgon (Also related to Lords of Thunder)
The Warrior Poet (St. John and de Gare)
Tender is the Knight (House of d'Vant)
Lord of Light
The Questing (related to The Dark Lord, Scorpion)
The Legend (House of Summerlin)

The Dragonblade Series: (Great Marcher Lords of de Lara)
Dragonblade
Island of Glass (House of St. Hever)
The Savage Curtain (Lords of Pembury)
The Fallen One (De Reyne Domination)
Fragments of Grace (House of St. Hever)
Lord of the Shadows

Queen of Lost Stars (House of St. Hever)

Lords of Thunder: The de Shera Brotherhood Trilogy
The Thunder Lord
The Thunder Warrior
The Thunder Knight

Highland Warriors of Munro:
The Red Lion
Deep Into Darkness

The House of Ashbourne:
Upon a Midnight Dream

The House of D'Aurilliac:
Valiant Chaos

The House of De Nerra:
The Falls of Erith
Vestiges of Valor

The House of De Dere:
Of Love and Legend

Time Travel Romance: (Saxon Lords of Hage)
The Crusader

Kingdom Come

<u>**Contemporary Romance:**</u>

Kathlyn Trent/Marcus Burton Series:
Valley of the Shadow
The Eden Factor
Canyon of the Sphinx

The American Heroes Series:
The Lucius Robe
Fires of Autumn
Evenshade
Sea of Dreams
Purgatory

Other Contemporary Romance:
Lady of Heaven
Darkling, I Listen
In the Dreaming Hour

Sons of Poseidon:
The Immortal Sea

<u>**Multi-author Collections/Anthologies:**</u>
Sirens of the Northern Seas (Viking romance)

Note: All Kathryn's novels are designed to be read as stand-alones, although many have cross-over characters or cross-over family groups. Novels that are grouped together have related characters or family groups.

Series are clearly marked. All series contain the same characters or family groups except the American Heroes Series, which is an anthology with unrelated characters.

There is NO particular chronological order for any of the novels because they can all be read as stand-alones, even the series.

For more information, find it in **A Reader's Guide to the Medieval World of Le Veque**.

Table of Contents

Prologue 1

Chapter One 8

Chapter Two 20

Chapter Three 30

Chapter Four 39

Epilogue 54

About Kathryn Le Veque 62

Prologue

1335 A.D.
Braelaw Manor
Stronghold of Clan Menzies near Collieston, Scotland

IT WAS A WIND-SWEPT DAY along the sea as the gulls cried overhead, riding the drafts. A storm was blowing in from the east and the vast and dark sea churned the waves until they shattered on the shore like broken glass.

Braelaw Manor was situated near the sea. The sounds of the smashing waves blowing across the sandstone walls created enough concern that the inhabitants were quickly putting things away, like animals and people and stores. Those who lived at Braelaw knew the sounds and smells of an approaching tempest and it was important to make sure everything was secured before the rain let loose.

"Jack! Lizelle!"

The children playing in the gray-colored sea grass outside of the open walls could hear their names being called. But it was fresh and cold out here, with the smell of the salt and the thrill of the oncoming storm. Jack had been distracted from his work when Lizelle, being the laird's daughter, had lured him out into the fields beyond, teasing him and chasing him as nine-year-old girls could do. Jack, at the grown-up age of twelve, was caught in that transition between manhood and boyhood, wanting to play but knowing he was too old for it. Lizelle was quite pretty and vivacious, and that stirred his young blood.

"Jack!"

Jackston Forbes heard his father's shout again and he knew he had to respond to it or he would be in for a painful lesson in why he should never ignore his father. As Lizelle ran circles around him, stopping only to drop flower petals on his auburn head, he finally turned for the manse.

"Jack!" Lizelle screamed, running up behind him. "Ye canna leave me! I'm a damsel about tae be swept out tae sea by a great sea monster!"

Jackston turned to look at her even as he continued to walk away. "I dunna see a sea monster."

Lizelle threw up her hands, spinning a circle and nearly falling over as she lost her balance. "Ye canna see him!" she declared. "He's magic!"

Jackston shook his head. "If I stop tae save ye, then someone will have tae save me from me da," he said. "He's a-callin' me."

Lizelle wouldn't be discouraged. Even as the wind picked up and began to seriously whip around them, scattering Lizelle's long blonde hair all about, she ran in front of Jackston to block his path.

"Ye canna go."

"I have tae go."

Lizelle put her hands on his chest, stopping his forward momentum. "Nay," she said, bossy. "Not until ye save me from the beast!"

Jackston knew he was going to be in trouble if he didn't make an appearance to his father very quickly. "I canna do it," he said, trying to move around her. "Let me pass."

Lizelle wouldn't. She refused. "Not until ye give me yer solemn oath."

"What oath?"

"That ye'll never save another lass from a monster, ever!"

"I promise."

"And that ye'll be true tae me always!"

Jackston liked Lizelle; he always had. She was full of life and lovely, if not spoiled and petty. But he found those traits humorous at times. Their families didn't live far from one another and his father did business with Lizelle's father with crossing stock of sheep and cattle.

Therefore, Jackston came to Braelaw about once every month or two with his father. And he and Lizelle always set off on some kind of adventure. Today it was sea monsters; last month, she was trapped in a castle –

although it was really a rock – and he was forced to battle a black knight in order to save her. Lizelle liked to be saved and saved often.

Truth be told, Jackston didn't mind. It made him feel rather dashing and daring, the faith she put in him. Therefore, when she asked for his vow, he gave it without hesitation.

"I promise, I'll always be true tae ye."

Lizelle flashed him a bright smile. "When we are older, ye will marry me, do ye hear? Ye canna marry another if ye've pledged tae be true tae me."

He shrugged. "As ye say."

Lizelle rushed up to stand in front of him, turning her head to show him her cheek. "Ye may kiss me, Jack."

Liking a lass was one thing. Kissing her was something completely different. "I willna do it," he said flatly, moving around her and moving quickly for the manse. "Come along now if ye dunna want tae feel a hand tae yer backside!"

He began to run and she followed, screaming his name all the way. He dashed inside the open front gates of the manse only to run headlong into his father, who was speaking to Lizelle's father. Jackston bashed into his father, Alexander, as Lizelle, running too fast to stop, crashed into the back of him.

"Here, now!" Alexander Forbes said. "What is the meanin' of this?"

Lizelle grabbed Jackston's hand and ran straight to her father, nearly yanking Jackston's arm out of his socket.

"Papa!" Lizelle cried. "Jackston has sworn tae be true tae me and he must marry me when we grow older! Tell him he must!"

Mortified, Jackston looked at Robert Menzies only to see the man gazing at his daughter with a rather confused expression.

"Marriage?" Robert repeated with some astonishment. "Ye're a bit young tae be speakin' of such things, lass."

Lizelle shook her head firmly. "He promised tae be true tae me," she insisted, looking at Jackston. "Dinna ye?"

Jackston was truly horrified and his freckled face turned as red as scarlet rose. "I… well, ye asked me tae be true and I… I said I would."

Robert could see how embarrassed the lad was. He grinned. "I willna hold ye tae a promise now, Jackston Forbes."

Lizelle's face fell. "But… but I want him tae marry me! He must, *he must!*"

She was becoming hysterical and Robert put his hands up to quiet her. "In time, lass. Ye're barely…."

"Papa, *please!*"

It was usually easier to give in to Lizelle than argue with her. Robert rolled his eyes as he looked at Jackston. "Come back in ten or fifteen years or she'll never shut her yap," he said impatiently. "But nothin' would give me more pleasure than tae have a Forbes for Lizelle. Ye're a fine lad."

Jackston had no idea what to say. The entire conversation baffled him. Alexander sensed his son's confusion and he came up behind the boy, putting a big hand on his son's skinny shoulder.

"He *is* a fine lad," Alexander said quietly. "And Lizelle is a fine lass. Mayhap we'll speak of a betrothal someday, but not today. I must get home before the storm hits."

Lizelle would not be refused. She tugged on her father's arm. "Make him say so, Papa! Make him say that Jackston will marry me!"

Robert cast an unhappy glance at his very spoiled daughter, his only child. She would inherit quite a fortune someday so he was very careful with any kind of marital commitment, as a man's word would be binding. It was even dangerous with what little he'd said so far if Alexander Forbes wanted to pursue it. And Alexander, as Lord Daviot, would be looking for a good marriage for his son, who would inherit the lordship someday.

Aye, they were on dangerous ground.

"Enough, Lizzie," Robert shushed her. "Go inside now."

"But –!"

"I'll not discuss this with ye now, ye silly lass. Go inside."

Lizelle wasn't particularly apt to obey her father even in the best of times. She looked right at Jackston, her lower lip trembling as the tears began to come.

"Ye said ye'd be true tae me," she said. "Did ye not mean it, then?"

Like most men, Jackston, even at his young age, couldn't stand to see a woman cry. Tears from a lass frightened him.

"I meant it," he assured her.

"Then ye'll marry me and no other?"

He hesitated and she burst into tears. "Aye, I will!' Jackston said simply to stop her outburst.

Lizelle's tears stopped unnaturally fast and she smiled triumphantly. "I knew ye would!" she gloated. She took off for the manse, her arms in the air in victory. "Jackston will marry me! He will!"

The three men watched her run off. Robert turned to Alexander apologetically. "She'll forget about it in a week," he said. "Dunna worry."

Alexander had to admit he was worried. Jackston had committed to something he should not have, but in his grasp, Jackston seemed quite calm about it.

"I suppose me da will have me marry when I get old," he said. "But I dunna want tae marry too soon. There are things I must do."

Robert was amused. "Like what?"

Jackston was a dreamer. He was also a lad of honor, of talent, and of great ambition. He had a purpose in life; he just didn't know what it was yet.

"I want tae travel," he said. "I want tae go tae England and learn the ways of the *Sassenach* knights. And then I want tae go tae Paris where the streets are made of marble, and I canna do that if I have a wife. She willna let me go."

Robert laughed softly, putting a hand on Jackston's head. "Wise lad," he said. "If ye find that ye still want tae marry Lizelle when ye return from all of the travelin' ye must do, then come and see me."

"Will ye make her wait for me, then?"

"If she has a mind tae."

That was good enough for Jackston. As he and his father went to gather their horses so they could return to their home of Blackbog Castle, about four miles to the west of Braelaw, Jackston couldn't help but think of the promise he'd made to Lizelle. He supposed she was as good as the next lass as far as a wife went. He would travel, he would learn things, and then he'd come home to her and make her marry him. She could give him sons and cook his meals, although something told him that Lizelle wouldn't be very good at cooking his meals. She might not even be very good at giving him sons, but without any other prospects, he was willing to take the chance.

After all... what more was there to a marriage that bearing children and making meals?

What *else* were women good for?

As Jackston pondered the role of a woman in his life, his horse was creating something of a distraction. He was a rather snippy pony who didn't like to be ridden at times. As Jackston and his father headed from the stables of Braelaw with the wide-open gates of the manse looming before them, Jackston's pony did a strange little dance and bolted as the wind whipped around him.

Jackston struggled to contain him, but to no avail. The pony ended up ramming into a group of people near the gate, including a little girl who was knocked down by the naughty animal. Chagrinned, Jackston leapt off the pony and pushed the beast back towards his father as a few hands were reaching down to pick up the child.

"Are ye hurt?" he asked the child anxiously. "I'm sorry about me pony. His name is Buckles. The wind frightens him sometimes."

The little girl, no more than five or six years of age, was trying to be brave. She was wiping her eyes furiously with the back of her hand while at the same time trying to get a look at her scraped elbow.

"I'm not hurt," she said.

Jackston could see the bloodied elbow and he felt very bad, indeed. But before he could say anything, the man that had pulled the little girl to her feet suddenly snatched her hand and yanked her away, heading off into the yard of the manse.

As the child was being pulled away, her gaze met with Jackston's and, for a moment, Jackston felt an odd sort of buzzing in his head. It was very strange. The child was a pretty little thing with big hazel eyes and an angelic little face. But she looked so sad, so incredibly sad, and that was perhaps why Jackston felt the buzzing in his head. As if he could feel the sorrow radiating from the child.

Perhaps it was the fact that his pony had hurt the girl. Or perhaps it was because the mean man had yanked her away. Or it was, perhaps, because Jackston always felt emotion far more than he should. For whatever reason, those hazel eyes stayed with Jackston as he and his father left the gates of Braelaw to make the trek back home before the storm set in with earnest.

As young as he was, Jackston was a lad with a heart. He was sensitive to people and emotions. It was something his father hated in him. Jackston tried to keep his emotions hidden away as his father did but, sometimes, he simply couldn't help it. Things like sorrow and anger affected him deeply. But those very feelings, the deep and emotional side of his soul, were things his mother encouraged.

Dunna be afraid tae feel things, Jackie, she would say. *Ye have an old soul. It tells ye things that others canna see.*

Conflicting instructions from his parents, something that kept him awake at night. He wanted to please them. Perhaps that was true what his mother said, that he had an old soul, but Jackston happy wasn't with it sometimes. It got him in trouble, like it did today when Lizelle cried and coerced him into saying he'd marry her. Well, he had to marry, anyway. But not before he was good and ready.

He just wasn't quite sure when that would be.

Chapter One

1348 A.D.
Blackbog Castle
Seat of the Lords of Daviot

"Jackie, ye canna run from it," Alexander scolded. "Ye should have never said ye'd marry the lass because her father heard ye had returned home and he wants ye tae come tae Braelaw."

Jackston was sitting at his mother's table in the hall of Blackbog Castle. Most men would say it was the father's table, but not Jackston. His mother ruled the house and hold, and his father was lucky that she permitted him to live there.

Even now, he sat at the old table, worn from years of use and repeated lye scrubbings, a great bowl of potage in front of him and about a half a loaf of bread with butter to break his morning fast. His mother had been feeding him all he could eat since he returned last week and swore if he kept this up, he was going to be as round as his father. But the food was good and he had missed it, so he shoveled cabbage and barley potage into his mouth.

"I'm not tryin' to run from anythin'," he told his father. "I'm simply not ready tae go tae Braelaw yet. I want tae see me friends up to the north still. I've not seen the lads at Springley yet."

Although Alexander loved his son dearly, he could see that the man didn't understand the seriousness of the situation. Why should he? He'd been a lad of thirteen years when he'd left home and headed to Dunster Castle, far away in the south of England. He'd fostered with the Sassenach branch of the Forbes family, cousins who had taught him the warring ways, and he'd spent the last several years in France. He'd even participated in the great battle at Crécy, a massive battle that had been a decisive victory for Edward III. Jackston had made a name for himself commanding an entire contingent of Welsh archers who had cut the French cavalry charges down again and again.

Word of Jackston Forbes' brilliance in the final charges of French knights was something that had spread back to England and all the way up into Scotland. When Alexander had first heard of his son's greatness from travelers heading north, he'd wept.

And he wanted his son to come home.

Two years later, Jackston appeared on his doorstep – older, meaner, far taller, and bulked out with muscles from having worked hard in his many years learning his skills as a knight. In fact, Alexander had hardly recognized the skinny lad he'd sent away because he received a very big man in return. The only thing that was the same was the auburn hair, now long and tied at the nape of his neck. And the eyes… eyes the color of amber, some would say. Intense, intelligent eyes. Those were the same, too.

But it was a man who had left things at home and had forgotten about them, his promise to Lizelle Menzies included. But that wasn't something Alexander could let him cast aside.

"The lads will have tae wait," Alexander said quietly, firmly. "I realize ye left here thirteen years ago and for ye, I'm sure nothin' of the past is a consideration for the future."

Jackston sighed heavily. "Da…."

Alexander cut him off. "I know ye've been off bein' the grand warrior for the past several years, but here at home, nothin' has changed. Everyone remembers ye as if it was just yesterday when they last saw ye, and that includes Robert Menzies. I still see him every few weeks and he still asks when ye're comin' home. I canna put the man off any longer because, sooner or later, someone is goin' tae tell him ye've come home. When he finds out ye've not gone tae see Lizelle, he's goin' tae want tae know why. What will ye tell him?"

By now, Jackston was growing frustrated. "Why does he want tae see me so badly?"

"Ye know why."

Jackston brushed him off. "For a vow I made thirteen years ago?"

"Aye."

"Does he truly plan tae hold me tae it?"

"He does."

Jackston was grossly unhappy now. "I was a child!"

"Mayhap. But ye made a man's vow. And if ye have any respect for this family and our name, ye'll face Robert Menzies. A man doesna so easily cast off a vow, Jackie. Ye made a promise."

Jackston leaned forward onto the table and put his face in his hands. His mother happened to enter the hall at that moment with more food for her son. But when she saw him with his hands covering his eyes, she nearly panicked.

"Jackie!" she cried. "What 'tis wrong?"

Jackston took his hands off of his face, sitting back as his mother put more food down in front of him. She then put her hand on his forehead to see if he was with fever.

"Are ye ill?"

"Nay, Lil."

Jackston's mother was Lilliana but he'd always, since childhood, called her "Lil" because that was what his father called her. Lilliana had grown to love hearing it from her son, expecting it. She'd missed it for all of these years.

"Did ye eat too much, then?" she asked anxiously.

Jackston laughed softly. "All I have done since returnin' home is eat."

"Then what is it?"

Jackston sighed again. "Da wants me tae go tae Braelaw and see Lizelle," he said. "He feels that since I told her, as a child, that I would marry her, that I must uphold me vow."

Lilliana fell quiet for a moment. "I know," she said. "Ye made a man's vow, Jackie."

Jackston looked at his father accusingly. "Did ye tell her tae say that?"

Alexander shook his head. "She knows what ye did," he said. "She's known for thirteen years. Look at yer mother, Jackie; would ye shame the woman by refusin' tae fulfill the vow ye made tae Lizelle? She willna say it but I will – if ye dunna do it, ye'll shame us all. I dunna care if ye've been a hero in battle. It matters naught if ye canna keep yer word."

Now he was being lectured on the honor of a knight, which was the last thing he wanted to hear. Jackston stood up, abruptly, and moved away from the table. The dogs that patrolled the hall followed him, hoping for a handout, but he ignored them as he faced his parents.

"So ye feel that any honor I've brought tae this family is erased if I dunna marry a girl I promised tae marry when I was a boy," he said angrily. "At the time, I thought I would marry her. But that was thirteen years ago and I've seen much of the world. I've seen happy marriages and unhappy marriages. I've seen a lot of things. I dunna know if Lizelle is still the wife I want tae have. Not everythin' of matter is in our own little world, ye know. There is more tae it than just this house, this little farm, and Lizelle Menzies."

Alexander could see that his son had grown far more worldly since the last he saw him. Not that he blamed him for refusing to fulfill a vow he'd made thirteen years ago. In a sense, he understood, but he was still coming to grips with the man who had shown up at his door last week. Jackston had grown in ways Alexander could have never had imagined, or understood, and with an outlook on life that was much different.

Some things, however, never changed no matter how worldly one was.

"Honor never changes," he said quietly. "All we have is our bond, lad. It's somethin' that canna be bought or sold, and the only person who can take it from us is, in fact, *us*. Ye made a promise, lad. If ye dunna intend tae keep it, then ye must go and tell Robert Menzies personally."

"Then I'll do that," Jackston said firmly. "I grow weary of yer guilt, tellin' me I'll shame the entire family if I dunna marry Lizelle. I will ride tae Braelaw today and we'll be done with this."

Alexander assumed as much; he'd never really held out much hope that Jackston would still want to marry Lizelle after all of these years. "At least go and see Lizelle," he said. "See if ye still want tae marry her. See if she is still the lass ye remember. But if she isna, then for our sake, be tactful with Robert. He's been me business partner for many a year. He admires you greatly."

Jackston didn't care if the man admired him greatly. He simply wanted to get this over with.

"Then I'll go," he said, turning for the entry of his family's home, which was really more of a fortified manor than an actual castle. The great hall, kitchen, and sleeping rooms were all built into one long building, arranged like a Norse longhouse, so his trek to the door was a lengthy one. "I'll go if only tae get this over with so I dunna have tae listen tae ye tell me I have no honor."

Alexander didn't say anything more. He was simply relieved his son was going to do his duty. Whether or not Jackston actually kept his vow was entirely up to Jackston; but at least if he didn't, he would face Robert Menzies like an honorable man and explain his reasons for declining.

Still, Alexander suspected that wasn't going to work out well. He knew that Lizelle hadn't entertained any suitors the entire time Jackston was away, going so far as to tell anyone who would listen that her betrothed was fighting wars in France. Nay, it wasn't going to go well at all if Jackston rejected her. The lass had been counting on this marriage for thirteen years and, like a dog with a meaty bone, she knew a good thing when she saw it.

She wasn't going to let it go.

Alexander found himself praying that Jackston's visit to Braelaw wouldn't result in losing a lifelong friend.

THE LAND WAS GREEN AND relatively dry, at least for the month of August, which made Jackston's trip to Braelaw a relatively quick and painless event. The topography was relatively flat with the exception of a hill now and again, flattening out as it drew closer to the sea. As Jackston and his steed, a big brown beast with hairy fetlocks known as Buckles the Fourth, or Bucky, loped easily down the dusty road, he kept thinking on the last time he'd come to Braelaw.

It had been right before he'd been sent south to Dunster Castle, a place where the world had opened up to him, far away from the narrow views of the north of Scotland. Fostering at Dunster and his subsequent service in

France had shown him how wide and terrible and wonderful the world was. He'd met more women than he could count and he'd even dallied with a few of them, and but when they wanted a commitment he refused to give, he would tell them of his betrothed in Scotland.

Aye, he would tell them of Lizelle. He wielded the woman like a shield between him and any female who wanted more from him than what he was willing to give. It was dastardly, to be truthful, because he really had no intention of keeping faith with his childhood vow to Lizelle although his parents thought differently. They were afraid that if he did not, then they would lose their honor. They would be shamed. Even though Jackston truly didn't want to marry Lizelle, he had to admit that his parents had a point. In this world, a man's word was everything and to break it meant he was a man without respect for himself or for others. And Jackston was far from that kind of men.

He'd learned a little something about honor in his years of training and battle. He, too, knew that honor was the most precious thing a man could own, something that could very well mean life or death to him. Therefore, it was with great reluctance that Jackston made his way to Braelaw, if for no other reason than to either talk or buy his way out of the betrothal.

If Robert Menzies would even permit it.

There was, therefore, some trepidation as he drew closer and closer to Braelaw. He didn't want to enter the gates only to be trapped by them. He was in the process of pondering his options of breaking out of the sealed manse when he began to hear sounds of a struggle.

He was nearing a heavily wooded area with a strip of water running through it and he could hear the distinct sounds of a struggle. His broadsword was by his left thigh and he drew it from its sheath, the brilliant steel reflecting the weak light. Pulling his horse to a slower trot, he listened carefully to see where, exactly, the sounds were coming from when a lad suddenly bolted across the road in front of him, carrying something in his hands.

Jackston's horse startled as four or five more figures came darting out in front of him, including a woman. She was running for the lad who had led the pack and it took Jackston a moment to realize that the lad was carrying a basket of some kind. Just as he reached the opposite side of the road, the woman leapt onto his back and sent him to the ground. Behind her, the other figures, which turned out to be more boys and young men, jumped on her. She began screaming and swinging her fists as the boys pawed at her.

That was all Jackston had to see. He spurred his war horse towards the scuffle and lifted his broadsword.

"*Enough*!" he roared. "Let the woman go! Woman, stop fightin'!"

The boys froze when they heard his voice but the woman didn't stop. She yanked the basket out of the boy's hands and slapped him in the head for good measure. But the boys didn't fight back; when they saw the big knight with the sword held high, they scattered like frightened rabbits. That left the woman seated on the road with the basket in her hands, looking disheveled.

Jackston pulled his steed alongside.

"Well?" he demanded. "What goes on here?"

The woman was out of breath; she had a kerchief around her head and was dressed in simple clothing, no more than a broadcloth skirt, a tunic, and a leather girdle tying it all together. She brushed the blonde hair out of her eyes, straightening her askew kerchief.

"I was gatherin' mushrooms, m'laird," she said, her voice trembling. "Those… those animals tried tae rob me."

Jackston looked off towards the west, where the boys had run, but he couldn't see them. They'd more than likely disappeared into the trees, burrowing deep, never to be found. He wasn't even really sure it was worth it to try.

"I see," he said. "Are ye injured?"

The woman shook her head. Then, she turned her face upwards to Jackston and he was immediately struck by big, hazel eyes. A tremor ran through him. Hadn't he seen those eyes before, set within that angelic face? Suddenly, he forgot all about the boys. He knew he'd seen the lass before but he couldn't quite place her.

"Do I know ye?" he asked, very curious. "I've seen ye before, I think."

The woman struggled to get to her feet, brushing off her skinned knees. "I… I dunna believe so, m'laird," she said.

"Where do you live?"

"Braelaw."

He cocked his head. "Is Robert Menzies yer master?"

She shook her head. "Nay, m'laird. Miss Lizelle is me mistress. These mushrooms are for her because she likes them so. She'll be very angry if I dunna bring enough back tae her and those lads tried tae steal them."

She was a lovely woman, if not on the skinny side, more than likely from inadequate nutrition. Her features were positively exquisite with her big eyes and long, blonde hair, now cluttered with dried grass and leaves from doing battle over her mushrooms. As Jackston watched her brush the dirt off her broadcloth skirt, it suddenly occurred to him where he'd seen her. The man had a mind like a steel trap and rarely forgot a face.

Now, he knew.

"The little lass!" he suddenly hissed. He pointed at her. "We met years ago when me pony knocked you down at Braelaw. Do ye not recall me?"

The woman was looking at him rather warily. "I... I'm sorry, but I dunna, m'laird."

Jackston wasn't satisfied with that answer. He sheathed his sword and dismounted the beast, standing in front of her as she continued to try and clean herself up.

"It was about thirteen years ago," he said. "I was leavin' Braelaw on me pony and he knocked ye down. Ye were a tiny lass at the time and there was a man with ye, a man who pulled ye away before I could properly apologize. Do ye mean tae tell me ye dunna remember that? Certainly, I look a bit differently. Time has a way of doin' that. But surely ye remember the incident."

She was peering at him strangely, trying very hard to recall what he was telling her. After a moment, her features seemed to ease.

"Was it a red pony?" she asked.

He grinned, triumphant. "Aye," he said. "That was me."

A look of relief came over her, as if she had been fearful what would have happened had she not remembered him. Because he was smiling, she timidly followed.

"I... I remember now," she said. "It was me first time at Braelaw. I'd never seen so many people."

He warmed to the conversation. "Where are ye from, lass?"

"Lonmay, m'laird," she said. "At least, I used tae be. I've lived at Braelaw since I was a wee bairn."

"Does yer family live there, then?"

Her smile faded. "Nay," she said, averting her gaze. "I was given over tae Laird Robert because me da owed him a debt. I've not seen me family since that time."

Jackston was coming to understand the situation somewhat. Servitude for a debt paid was not uncommon. "Ye were quite a small lass the day I saw ye at Braelaw, as I recall."

She nodded. "That was the last time I ever saw me da."

"How old were ye?"

She looked up at him, then. "I dunna know, m'laird," she said. "I was never learned."

"Ye mean ye dunna know how tae read or write?"

"Nay, m'laird."

So she had been a servant her entire life. She didn't have to know anything more than what her duties entailed, like picking mushrooms for her mistress. Jackston wasn't surprised to find her uneducated but he did think it to be a shame. She was a truly beautiful woman and he'd seen enough to know. That kind of beauty was rare. It seemed to him that she was being wasted as a servant. Someone of her comely looks would do far better on the arm of a soldier or a knight even.

There was something about her that suggested she deserved better.

"Well," he said, pointing to the basket. "If ye're done with yer gatherin', I'll take ye back tae Braelaw. I'm heading there meself."

She looked down at her basket, only half-full, and sighed. "I had so many that were knocked from the basket by those lads," she said as she headed back across the road. "I must find what I dropped or Miss Lizzie will be very angry."

Leaving his steed to munch on the thick green grass by the side of the road, Jackston followed the woman back into the trees on the other side. She dropped to her knees and began picking up all manner of mushrooms that had scattered over the ground as the result of her struggle against the mushroom thieves.

Jackston simply stood there beneath the cool canopy and watched her for a moment before realizing there were a few mushrooms by his feet. He bent over and picked them up, dropping them into her basket. Then he saw a few more so he went to pick those up as well.

"Do ye always come here to pick mushrooms?" he asked. "'Tis a far sight away from Braelaw."

She nodded, looking around at her feet to find a few more. "Aye," she said. "Most of the time Miss Lizzie comes with me, but today she dinna because her betrothed is comin' tae visit. She wants tae greet him properly."

Betrothed. She meant him. Jackston felt that familiar surge of reluctance at the mention. The fact that Lizelle was waiting for him, like the spider for the fly, only served to increase his hesitation. If he was a smart man, he'd simply turn tail for England and never look back. But honor, and his parents' respect, meant more to him at the moment.

But he wondered for how much longer.

"It looks as if ye've found most of yer missin' mushrooms," he pointed out, changing the subject. "Have ye ever run into those lads before?"

"Nay," she said, sounding frustrated. "But I ever see them again, I'll give them a fist tae the face. I would have done it had ye not intervened."

Jackston laughed softly. "I believe ye," he said. "In fact, ye were fightin' the whole lot of them when I saw ye. That's very brave."

She grinned, modestly. "I've always had a bit of a temper," she admitted. "Especially since I have no desire tae be beaten for not bringin' enough mushrooms back tae Braelaw."

His smile faded unnaturally fast. "Who would beat ye for that?"

She bent over to pick up the last mushroom. "Miss Lizzie has a bit of the temper, too," she said. Then, her head shot up and her eyes widened. "I dinna mean tae say anythin' badly about her. She's a good lady, she is. Please dunna tell her I said so about the temper!"

She almost seemed in a panic and Jackston shook his head. "I willna tell her," he said. But her reaction to Lizelle gave him a hint of who, in fact, was doing the beating. He wasn't sure he liked that. "What is yer name, lass? I never even asked ye."

She seemed to breathe a sigh of relief that he would not repeat what she'd said. "Rora," she said. "I am Rora of Lonmay."

He bowed before her. "Rora of Lonmay," he greeted. "'Tis a pleasure tae meet ye. Will ye allow me tae accompany ye back tae Braelaw?"

"It would be most appreciated, m'laird." She cocked her head, looking at him in a way that made his heart leap strangely. Her eyes, those brilliant things, were riveted to him, dissecting him. "Ye speak differently than the men around here. May I ask where ye're from?"

He reached out and took the basket from her as he began to find his way out of the bushes and back towards his horse. "I am from Blackbog, which is not far from here," he told her, "but I've spent many a year in England and France."

Rora followed him, seemingly quite interested. "'Tis a wonderful thing," she said. "Did ye like those places?"

"I did."

"What did ye do when ye were there?"

He shrugged as they crossed the road. "Learned how tae fight," he said. "I fought battles for kings."

Rora was duly impressed. "Sometimes travelers stop at Braelaw," she said. "We've heard tale of wars in France. Did ye hear of them?"

"I was in them."

"Ye *were*?" she gasped in awe. "What did ye do? I mean, did ye fight against the French king?"

Jackston nodded. "I did," he said. "And I won."

"Then ye must be a great warrior, indeed."

He reached his horse and handed the basket of mushrooms back to her. "I am, mayhap, the greatest warrior in all of Scotland," he said, feigning arrogance. "Ye can tell everyone that ye met the great Jackston Forbes and they will be very impressed."

Rora suddenly came to a halt, looking at him with a mixture of disappointment and surprise. "Jackston," she murmured. "Ye… ye're Jackston?"

He was amused at her expression. "Aye," he said. "Have ye heard of me, then?"

She nodded. "Ye're Miss Lizelle's Jackston."

His smile faded. Somehow, he just didn't like hearing that from her lips. *Lizzie's Jackston*. Nay, he wasn't Lizelle's Jackston, not yet. Maybe not even ever. Hearing that statement from Rora made him truly hate the entire idea. Putting a booted foot in the stirrup, he mounted his steed.

"I have known Lizelle since we were children," he told her, reaching down a hand to pull her up effortlessly onto the saddle behind him. "I am simply goin' to visit her, as me parents have requested."

Rora didn't say anything as she settled in behind Jackston and he gathered his reins. When he directed the horse out onto the road and the animal did a bit of a skip, the arm that wasn't holding the basket of mushrooms suddenly went around his torso, holding on so she wouldn't fall off.

Jackston felt her arm around him and he rather liked it. Truth be told, he rather liked her, although he wasn't sure why. Something about those magnificent eyes captivated him, a simple woman who was brave and curious.

A servant girl he had no business being attracted to.

Perhaps it was his last stab at resisting Lizelle, finding the woman's servant attractive. A warrior of his caliber would take a servant girl like Rora to his bed and nothing more. A relationship of any kind or marriage was strictly forbidden. In fact, it wasn't such a bad idea to take Rora to his bed, finding sport with this beautiful woman, but something in him couldn't quite go that far.

In spite of what his father said, he had a great deal of honor and more scruples than most. The one thing that would keep him from admitting this lass to his bed was the fact that he couldn't quite get over the way she made him feel.

Like nothing he'd ever felt before.

Those eyes. Jackston was used to his infatuations being a hollow thing, something that didn't fulfill him. But this beautiful young servant girl – a lass he remembered from the first time he ever saw her – did something to him when she looked at him. Was it witchcraft? Was it foolery?

He wondered.

All he knew was that something about that woman gripped him. And he had no idea why.

Chapter Two

Within a few minutes of announcing his arrival to the men manning the gates of Braelaw, Jackston felt like he was a returning emperor.

Dropping Rora off at the gates, his attention was still riveted to her even as she scurried away, disappearing around the side of the manse and into the kitchen yard. But he was soon distracted by Robert Menzies himself, who came forth from the manse with his arms open wide as if to embrace a long-lost son.

But that was just the beginning. Jackston found himself embraced and praised, fawned over by Robert and a few members of his household, including an older woman introduced to him as Robert's spinster sister.

But, oh… did the woman have an eye for Jackston! He smiled weakly at her and she winked boldly at him, batting her eyes and generally making a spectacle of herself. Jackston would have laughed had he not been so dismayed. And rather frightened. So he tried to ignore the woman with the smooth, red cheeks and no eyebrows as Robert pulled him towards the manse, announcing to everyone around them that Lizelle's Jackston had finally returned.

Lizelle's Jackston!

There was that phrase again, but the welcome at Braelaw was far more of a welcome than Jackston had even received at his own home. Still, there hadn't been an old spinster desperately attempting to flirt with him. So, he kept his eyes off the woman, instead focusing on Robert and the fact that the man was truly trying to give him a warm welcome. He appreciated it. He appreciated it more when Robert pulled him into the hall of the manse and plied him with expensive wine and sweets.

Even with the wine in him, he still wasn't apt to respond to the spinster, who had planted herself beside him and even rubbed her foot against his leg under the table. Jackston thought it was all rather bold, crazily so, and he ignored the woman soundly as Robert stood on the other side of the table and praised Jackston for his prowess in battle and for honoring them all with his great reputation.

Jackston soaked up the accolades, feeling rather full of himself, but he eventually grew weary of the spinster who was now trying to put her hand on his thigh, still under the table and away from her brother's view. When she actually pinched his leg, he "accidentally" spilled a half-cup of that beautiful red wine onto the woman's robes, which had the desired effect. Bolting up from the table as Jackston apologized for his clumsiness, the spinster fled the chamber to change her clothing and Jackston had a reprieve.

Or did he…?

As the spinster quit the hall in a fluster, Lizelle entered from the opposite end. Her entrance, Jackston was sure, was meant for maximum impact because she entered the chamber in a beautiful pink gown, surrounded by two women who held the ends of the gown up so it wouldn't drag on the dirty floor. With a bouquet of buttercups in her hand, wild flowers that bloomed this time of year, she held them to her face, smelling them, so that only her eyes were visible.

Somewhere behind Lizelle, Jackston could hear a lyre. *God's Bones, someone is playing music for her entrance!* he thought. He almost burst out laughing at the sheer showmanship of it, finding it very hard not to even smile as Lizelle entered the hall with her women and her own musician. He put a hand over his mouth, in fact, pretending to wipe any crumbs or remnants of wine away, but the truth was that he found the pomp ridiculous. In hindsight, that should have been a foretaste of things to come.

He should have considered himself warned.

As Lizelle drew near the table, Jackston took a close look at her as she lowered the bouquet from her nose; she was still lovely but somewhere in the years, her face had elongated and her teeth had grown in, becoming slightly protruding. Her eyes were still the same pure shade of blue and her blonde hair was very long, to her knees, and unbound to display her maiden status. When her gaze met Jackston's, she smiled with her unnaturally big teeth.

"Ye have finally come," she sighed happily, her gaze dragging up and down his body. "I have dreamt of this day, Jackston. For many a year, I've dreamt of ye and prayed ye would return tae me whole and sound. Ye've grown intae a comely lad with big muscles and a powerful look about ye. I dinna believe ye would return tae me so handsome."

Jackston knew, instinctively, that she was looking for a similar reply. He cleared his throat softly. "And ye're still lovely, Lizelle," he said, watching her beam. "Have… have ye been well?"

Lizelle nodded eagerly. "I have," she said. "Oh, Jackston, it is so good tae see ye again. I thought about ye every day that ye were gone. Did ye think of me, at least sometimes?"

Only when I was tryin' to fend off a woman who wanted more from me than I was willin' to give, he thought. "Aye," he replied steadily. "I did."

It wasn't a lie.

Lizelle swooped on him, wrapping both of her arms around his left arm, her hands sliding into his big calloused one. "I am so pleased tae hear that," she said. Then, she was pulling on him. "Come with me. We must become reacquainted with each other now. I want tae hear about yer adventures fightin' in France."

Jackston had no choice but to follow her as she dragged him from the hall and down a short corridor. There were stairs there, mural stairs that folded back on themselves as they led to the floor above, and he followed her as she pulled him up. He couldn't help but notice her women were following, older ladies in severe wimples, and that damnable lyre player was bringing up the rear.

Strains from gut strings followed him up the stairs. It would have been comical had he not been so annoyed by it. But Lizelle smiled hugely at him, her hands wrapped all around his left arm as she dragged her victim to a small chamber on the second floor that was strewn with all manner of things for a lady's entertainment – a larger harp was propped against the wall and near the window was an easel with a framed stretch of vellum. A palette of paints lay on a table next to it.

Once in the chamber, Lizelle directed Jackston to a chair and politely asked him to sit. He did, watching Lizelle and her women as they scampered around the room, bumping into each other as they went to light fires and pour wine. Lizelle shoved a cup of wine into his hand, a very lovely painted cup, and then she sat down next to him and promptly collected a piece of sewing.

"Now," she said, collecting her needle. "Ye will tell me about yer adventures in France. I want to hear everythin'."

Frankly, Jackston was still a little flabbergasted by it all; with the ridiculous harp player in the corner of the room, strumming on his strings, a fire in the hearth, and Lizelle settling down with her sewing, she was creating quite a domestic scene. Jackston knew it was intentional; she wanted him to see what his life with her would be like – harp players, efficient servants, wine, and an obedient wife. She wanted him to see how wonderful it would be. Aye, the move was quite calculated. But at that moment, he wanted nothing more than to run screaming from the chamber.

Honor, he kept telling himself. *Think of yer parents' honor*!

"Well," he began, "I havena been in France all this time. When I left after last ye saw me, I want tae Dunster Castle in Devon. Me cousins live there. 'Twas there I trained as a knight and learned the ways of the Sassenach warrior."

Lizelle was stitching intently but still listening to him with great interest. "Were ye knighted, then?"

"Aye."

She smiled that broad, toothy smile. "What a prideful thing!" she exclaimed. "I dunna know another knight, not in all of the north!"

He shrugged. "There are many fine warriors in the north," he said. "I am not the only one."

She put her hand on his arm; she had pretty hands. "But I dunna know another who has distinguished himself in battle as ye have," she insisted. "We heard tale of the battles in France against the French king. A merchant travelin' north tae Aberdeen stopped one night and told us all about

Edward's armies and how they were victorious, and how a Forbes knight in charge of archers helped turn the tides of the battle at Crécy. Jackston Forbes, he said!"

Jackston cleared his throat in a modest gesture. "It was the command I was given," he said. "I did what I had tae do."

Lizelle was so proud that she was nearly bursting with it. "Ye've become a great man, Jackie," she said. "It has made me very happy. I've told everyone how ye vowed tae marry me upon yer return. It has been the most prideful thing of me life."

Jackston looked at her, seeing her beaming face and knowing that he wasn't feeling the same way she was. He'd spent the past several years growing up and becoming a man; she'd spent the last several years at Braelaw dreaming of his return. He *was* her world, or at least a very large component of it. He could see it by simply looking at her. Guilt and distaste began to sweep him.

What have I gotten meself intae?

"What have ye done since I have been away?" he asked because he utterly wanted off the subject of marriage. "Have ye kept busy? And how is yer father? I've not had much chance tae speak with him."

Lizelle returned to her sewing. "Me da and yer da have kept company frequently," she said. "They play board games and they hunt regularly together. 'Twill be wonderful for them both when their children have married. We will be a great happy family."

She wasn't willing to move away from the subject of marriage, at least not yet. Jackston was starting to feel manipulated, so he tried another tactic.

"Do ye mean tae tell me that ye havena entertained not one suitor since I've been gone?" he asked, trying to sound as if he was jesting but he was afraid he was coming across as sounding desperate. "Surely young men have come tae call for ye, Lizelle. Ye're a pretty woman with wealth. That would attract many a man."

She flushed, her cheeks turning pink. "Of course not," she insisted. "I am betrothed. Why would I entertain suitors?"

"Not one?"

"Not one!"

So much for that avenue. Jackston noticed the cup of wine still in his hand and he downed the entire thing in three big swallows. His empty cup was a magnet to one of the female servants, who rushed forward with more wine, something he gladly accepted. He had a feeling he was going to need it.

"Tell me more about what ye have done whilst I was gone," he said glumly, downing another big swallow of wine.

Lizelle was still sewing primly. "Life at Braelaw has been uneventful," she said. "We had some bad winters not long ago and me da lost some of his herd, but yer da was kind enough tae help him. Our families have been very close since ye've been away. And what about ye? Did ye find any other women pretty whilst ye were away from me?"

The woman only sang two notes – marriage and the closeness of their families. He couldn't seem to deter her from either. As the wine began to fill his veins, Jackston was becoming increasingly unhappy. The more he looked at Lizelle and what she represented – a home with many possessions, ladies-in-waiting, a lyre player following her from room to room to set music to her procession, the more that wasn't what he wanted in life. He intended to return south to Dunster Castle. He wanted to continue on as a knight, serving with his family to the south, making a name for himself as a warrior and as a man, and what Lizelle represented… well, he just didn't want any part of it or any part of her. It really wasn't her fault – he'd just outgrown her.

He wanted his own life, *his* way.

He must have delayed too much on answering her question because she stopped sewing and looked up at him with a clearly distressed expression. Quickly, he spoke.

"The world is full of pretty women," he said. "Did I find any like ye? Nay, I dinna. Ye're unique tae Braelaw, a lass I remember from me childhood."

It was as pleasing an answer as he could come up with but she was clearly flattered by it. Her smile returned and she lowered her eyes modestly to her sewing once more.

"I'm glad," she said. "I dunna know what I would do if ye found company with another. But let us not speak of it; ye're home and now… now, what shall we do?"

He knew exactly what she meant. God's Bones, there was no question in his mind. Could he tell her that he'd reconsidered their marriage? Could he tell her that he'd made a vow as a child and he'd had no idea of what he was committing to? Certainly, he *could* tell her, but he knew she wouldn't understand.

With her question, the lass was looking for information on when he intended they should be wed. There was no way he could marry her but, for the sake of his parents, he had to let her down easy. He had to make it seem as if, perchance, *he* was the unattractive marital prospect. If this betrothal had any chance of being broken, then it would have to come from her so he could, in his father's words, keep his honor. But… what to say?

What to say?

Thankfully, he was interrupted when a figure hustled in through the solar door, a small figure in a broadcloth skirt and a kerchief on her head. Jackston recognized Rora immediately and his heart leapt at the sight. God, he was happy to see her, but struggled not to react in any way. In fact, he had to force himself to look away, fearful that his joy to see her would be written all over his face. Then, he wouldn't have to tell Lizelle anything because she would know what was in his heart. That little servant girl with the enormous eyes had his attention.

The forbidden little lass.

Quickly, he turned away, rising from his chair and moving over to the window where he could take a breath of fresh air. He leaned against the sill, turning his head slightly so he could watch Rora as she went straight to Lizelle with the tray she was carrying, a tray of edibles for the lady and her guest.

But Jackston noticed something interesting at that point; Lizelle was very sharp with Rora. Sharp of movement, of command, right from the onset. Treating the servant as if she were no better than dirt. Rora set the tray down on a delicate painted table next to her mistress, but Lizelle sharply ordered the girl to move it away, to the bigger table in the room. Rora obediently did that and Lizelle set her sewing aside, standing up to go to the tray and see what was upon it.

That's when the trouble really started. Jackston wasn't really sure what was meant to be on the tray, but whatever had been brought didn't please the mistress. Lizelle commanded Rora to take the tray away and bring back a correctly-laden tray, a brusque order that Rora quietly obeyed.

Jackston found himself curious about the way Lizelle spoke to Rora because he remembered Rora's intimation that Lizelle beat her. From the way Lizelle was treating the lass, he was coming to see that it was something he could easily believe. In fact, Lizelle was becoming increasingly hostile with Rora and, as Jackston watched, suddenly reached out and grabbed the girl's arm as if to shake her. But that action caused Rora to dump the tray on Lizelle's pink dress, and Lizelle screeched as she brought up a hand and slapped Rora across the face with an open palm. She then shoved the girl down to her knees and demanded she pick up the food, all the while lamenting her dirty dress. Jackston came away from the wall.

"Here, now," he said, frowning at Lizelle. "Why did ye do that?"

Lizelle was furious. "The clumsy fool!" she cried. "Look what she did to me gown! It is ruined!"

Jackston could see the stains on the front of the pink brocade. "It seems tae me that ye caused that yerself," he said. "I saw ye grab the lass by the arm, Lizelle. What happened was not her fault."

Lizelle's eyes widened at him, utterly shocked that he should side with the servant. Down on the floor, still picking up the food that had fallen, Rora suddenly lifted her head.

"Nay, m'laird," she insisted, sounding terrified. "It 'twas me own fault. I am very sorry tae have ruined everythin'. I am very clumsy!"

She sounded so bloody scared. Anger flared in Jackston's chest. Before he could reply, one of Lizelle's women reached down and yanked Rora to her feet, practically tossing her from the room as the second woman picked up the tray and tossed it out of the door after her. Jackston could hear the tray clattering, the food, no doubt, spraying on Rora. He stood there, open-mouthed, as Lizelle's women slammed the chamber door and then rushed to Lizelle to see the damage to her dress.

Jackston had to step away; he was furious with what he'd just witnessed but he was wise enough to keep his mouth shut. He suspected, from Rora's reaction, that it wouldn't go particularly well in her favor if he took her side. It was just a feeling he had. It seemed that Lizelle was very hostile towards her pretty young servant and that had been evident from the moment Rora had entered the chamber. As Lizelle practically wept to the women who were trying to brush the stains off her skirt, Jackston leaned back against the wall.

"Is that how ye treat yer servants, Lizelle?" he asked evenly. "Truly? Do ye actually take a hand tae them in front of others?"

Lizelle looked at him, mortified. "She… she is a stupid girl," she stammered. "For her to spill on me…."

"Ye shook her by the arm. Ye caused her tae spill. I saw it."

Now, Lizelle was turning red in the face. "If she had obeyed me orders from the first, I wouldna had tae punish her," she said, struggling to justify her actions. "She was tae bring bread and cheese and pickled mushrooms. She dinna bring the cheese I requested."

"Did ye ask her why?"

"It doesna matter why!"

"Did ye ask her *why*?"

Lizelle was clearly flustered. "She said there was none in the kitchens, but I know that not tae be true!"

"How do ye know? Do ye spend much time in the kitchens that ye would know that?"

Utterly rattled, Lizelle gathered her skirts and pushed her women out of the way. "I must change me clothes," she said. Then, she started to weep angrily. "I wanted this tae be so nice. We havena seen each other in years and I so wanted this tae be perfect. I am sorry it wasna. If ye'll give me a little time, I'll change me dress and come right back. Mayhap we can… try again?"

Jackston didn't want to try again. He'd seen a flash of Lizelle's true self in her behavior with Rora and he could see that she was still the petty, spoiled girl he'd left those years ago. Behavior he'd once thought entertaining he now thought appalling. In fairness, it could have been because he felt an odd sense of protection over Rora and Lizelle's brutality had him more agitated than he should have been. In truth, he really didn't know why. All he knew was that he had to get clear of the woman and think about what he really wanted to do.

Did he want to take the time to discourage her from the marriage? Or did he simply want to tell her he had no intention of keeping his vow and let the situation take its natural course. Whatever the case, he was glad to be free of her for the moment.

"Go," he waved a hand at her, turning back to the windowsill and the sea breezes beyond.

"Ye willna leave?"

He hesitated. "I willna leave."

He spoke the words begrudgingly but that was enough for Lizelle. Satisfied, she scurried off with her women, leaving Jackston alone in her solar with the lyre player still strumming in the corner. He glanced at the musician, who was seemingly lost in his own world, and knew he needed to get out of there. A place like this – a woman's solar – was no place for him.

Swiftly, he quit the chamber and made his way out of the manse.

Chapter Three

ONCE JACKSTON LEFT THE MANSE, he made it as far as the stables. There, he came to a halt. His steed was in one of the stalls, munching happily on the grain provided, and Jackston wandered over to the beast, affectionately slapping the big rump. All the while, however, his mind was whirling with what he'd just witnessed – Lizelle's behavior, Rora's reaction, his own feelings in general. All of it was spinning around in his mind so that it was difficult to isolate just one thought. They were all related, all tied up together, and he could hardly make sense of them.

Do I marry Lizelle as I once promised to do?

Or do I forsake me parents' honor and run?

More and more, he simply didn't want to be bothered with this. He didn't want to marry Lizelle but didn't possess the patience any longer to make a game out of it so she would be the one to refuse the betrothal. Now, he simply wanted to leave and never look back. He couldn't envision himself married to a woman he may have been fond of once, but distance and time had reduced that fondness to indifference. With a mean streak in her, Lizelle wasn't anyone he wanted to be saddled with.

Perhaps the best thing to do was simply speak with her father and be honest.

Surely Robert Menzies knew that his daughter was a spoiled shrew. Surely he would understand if Jackston explained that the vow he'd once given to marry her was a child's vow, something he'd given and had no idea of the seriousness of it. But remembering the welcome he'd been given by Robert, Jackston was coming to seriously doubt the man would take it well if

Jackston told him he had no intention of marrying his daughter. In fact, it might crush Robert more than it would crush Lizelle. He was coming to think that Robert wanted his daughter married simply so she would cease to be his problem any longer.

God's Bones... what would he do if Robert begged him to take her off his hands?

And then there was Rora....

Beautiful, simple, sweet... he didn't even really know the lass, but what he did know of her, he liked. And not in a lustful sense, either, which was unusual with him. There was something very strong yet incredibly fragile about Rora, an allure he'd never before experienced. But the fact that she was a servant... it wasn't something he could pursue with her.

... or was it?

He was planning on returning to England, anyway. What if... what *if* he were to take her with him? No one would know she had only been a servant. She was finer and more beautiful than any noblewoman he'd ever known, angelic to a fault. It would be easy to believe she was bred from fine stock.

But for what purpose would he take her with him? To marry her? To simply take sport with her?

He really wasn't sure.

Someone entered the stable at that point, distracting him, and he glanced up from his horse's rump to see that Rora had made an appearance. The sunbeams streaming in from the ventilation windows high on the walls caught her hair, glistening off of it, and Jackston stood straight as she entered, drinking in the sight of her. Their eyes met as she scampered in his direction.

"I-I saw ye leave the manse, m'laird," she said before he could speak. She was breathless, as if she'd been running. "I wanted tae thank ye for speakin' up for me to Miss Lizelle. It was very noble."

He smiled at her. "It was the truth."

"Ye musna do it again."

His smile faded. "Why not?"

She sighed heavily, an expression of pain and fear crossing her features. "Because she will only take it out on me," she said quietly. "Miss Lizelle...

she doesna like it when her word is challenged."

Jackston could see that was true. He eyed Rora a moment before taking a few steps over to the stable wall, sliding down to his buttocks. He patted the hard-packed earth next to him.

"Come here, lass," he said. "Sit down. I want tae speak tae ye."

Obediently, Rora went to sit next to him, a proper distance between them. She looked at him, wide-eyed and expectant, and he found himself studying the lines of her face. She was quite fascinating to look at. He could also see the nearly perfect handprint on the left side of her cheek and neck from where Lizelle had struck her. That brought his anger about all over again.

"How long has she been treating ye so poorly?" he asked.

Rora lowered her gaze. "Oh…," she said, shrugging faintly, "I dunna know. I have been her servant since I was very young. It is simply her way."

Jackston didn't like that answer. "It is not a good way," he said. "Do you understand that?"

She looked up at him. "It doesna matter. I have no say in what she does."

That was very true. But Jackston didn't like to hear that. "I know ye dunna, but does her father ever say anythin'? Surely Robert doesna approve of the way she treats her servants."

Rora shrugged. "The laird keeps tae himself. Miss Lizelle does as she pleases." She paused a moment, looking at Jackston in a way that suggested she had no idea why he was concerned for her. "Miss Lizelle isna always as ye see. Sometimes, she can be kind. But kindness is not truly who she is."

"What do ye mean?"

Rora cocked her head thoughtfully. "I mean that we all have things we keep hidden, that we dunna want others tae see," she said. "It is who we truly are, our hidden heart, and most of us keep it buried. Miss Lizelle's hidden heart is full of fear and cruelty. She is afraid of many things, and that fear causes her tae become cruel. She has been speakin' of yer visit for years and today, she was a-feared it would be ruined so her cruelty came out."

It was an astonishingly insightful analysis from a woman who lived a simple life of servitude. No education, no real opportunity to expand her mind, yet Rora had a grasp of things few people did. That impressed him greatly.

"And ye?" he asked quietly. "What is yer hidden heart?"

Rora smiled bashfully. "I've never given much thought tae it."

He smiled because she was, his gaze drinking in every movement, every flutter of her eyelashes. "Then let me tell ye," he said. "I suspect yer hidden heart is one of patience and compassion, for it is a rare woman that would see inside others like that. I sense that ye feel some pity for Lizelle."

The warm expression on Rora's face faded. "She is unhappy."

"Why?"

Rora shook her head. "A lot of reasons, I think," she said. "But it wouldna do for me tae tell ye. That is somethin' she must tell ye herself."

He respected the fact that she wasn't going to gossip about her mistress. He leaned back against the wall, his gaze still lingering on her as if he were incapable of looking at anything else. He found that he wanted to know more about this insightful young woman he was so attracted to.

"Ye're correct," he said. "If anyone is tae do the tellin', it should be her. But I dunna want tae talk about her anymore. I want tae talk about ye. Ye told me that yer da sold ye tae Robert Menzies in payment for a debt."

Rora nodded. "Aye."

"Tell me about yer family. I want tae hear of yer people."

She considered his question. "There isna much tae tell," she said. "Me family is from Lonmay, tae the north. Me da is a smithy but he wanted tae try his luck with a herd of cattle. He did some work for Laird Robert and asked for a loan of money. Laird Robert wouldna give him a loan, so me da sold me tae Laird Robert for the money. I have three brothers, ye see, and bein' the only lass, I suppose he did the only thing he could tae get the money he needed."

Jackston was listening intently. "So he sold ye."

She nodded. "Aye," she said. "Me ma was dead these many years and I suppose me da had no use for me."

She spoke as if using her as a business transaction was of no consequence. Of course, transactions like that happened all of the time, but still, there was something cold about selling flesh and blood. Jackston shook his head. "I'm not sure I could sell me daughter," he said. "Seems like a harsh thing tae do."

Rora didn't see his point. "Why?" she asked. "I live in a big house. I have a bed tae sleep in and food tae eat. I'm not sad for what me da did. I am in a better place."

Jackston was touched by her optimism. "Ye're in a place where yer mistress beats ye," he said, reaching out to grasp her chin gently and turn her face to get a look at the handprint on her skin. "Truly, Rora… ye have a brighter outlook on life than I would in the same situation. It doesna quite seem fair."

His touch seemed to do something to her; Rora's breathing seemed to come faster, her full bosom heaving gently beneath her tunic. "Nothin' in life is truly fair," she said, trembling as he ran a finger over the red welt. "But I am more fortunate than most. I thank God that I have a warm bed and good food. And… and I hope not tae be here forever."

He dropped his hand from her face although it was difficult; he was fighting the urge to pull the woman into his arms. That silken skin and lips the color of a ripe peach were calling to him.

"Is that so?" he asked, simply to distract himself. "Where do ye plan tae go?"

She looked at him, smiling. "Somewhere far away," she said, her expression taking on a somewhat dreamy countenance. "Can…can I tell ye a secret?"

"Of course."

"Ye willna tell Miss Lizelle?"

"Never."

She bit her lip in a gesture that suggested she was about to lay forth a tremendous secret. "There are travelers that stop here sometimes," she said. "I listen tae them speakin' in the hall, tellin' tales of their travels. Sometimes… sometimes I hope that Laird Robert will sell me tae one of these merchants so that I can travel with them. I want tae go tae London and Paris, or even Rome. I heard a man say that all of Rome is built with golden pillars. It seems tae me that tae travel tae a place like that would be just like goin' tae heaven."

He was grinning. "And ye want tae see that?"

She nodded eagerly. "I do," she said. "Very much."

Jackston had to admit that she had him fairly enchanted by this point. Not only was she a beautiful woman, but she was intelligent and had ambition. He found that a fascinating combination. Unlike Lizelle, who was content to sit in her solar and rot, Rora had dreams. She wanted to learn, to see, to grow. Jackston liked that a great deal.

"Then I hope yer dreams come true," he said. "I have dreams meself."

Now it was her turn to be fascinated. "Ye do?" she asked. "But I heard that ye were a great knight. Surely, ye've lived yer dreams."

He shook his head. "Not nearly enough," he said. "Surely, I have seen a lot. I have accomplished quite a bit. But there is much more tae life and I want tae see and do all I can before it's over with."

Rora smiled at the appeal of living fully. "As do I," she said. "I wish ye good fortune, then, in doin' all ye wish tae do."

"I wish ye the same."

They gazed at each other for a moment and Jackston could feel the warmth between them. He was hoping it wasn't imagination on his part because he was attracted to the little servant as he'd never been attracted to anyone in his life. There was so much more to her than most women he'd met, something sweet and alluring. What was it he'd said about her hidden heart? Truth be told, there was much more than patience and compassion there. Much, much more. But they were all things she kept tucked far away.

She was close enough to grab and he did so, reaching out to cup her sweet face as his lips slanted over hers. That urge he'd been fighting since she came into the stable overwhelmed him until it was no longer something he could ignore. He had to taste her, at least once, to know what he would be forever missing. A forbidden kiss and nothing more. He would be satisfied and, perhaps, not so infatuated with her.

Unfortunately, his attempt to taste something forbidden worked against him.

He wanted more.

Pulling Rora into his arms, his kisses became more insistent. His tongue licked at her, gently prying her lips apart and snaking into her mouth. Against him, Rora had collapsed completely, overwhelmed by his strength and his power. She hadn't resisted at all. But the truth was that she was a servant and if a man above her station had a mind to take her, then she didn't have much say in it.

That thought ran through Jackston's mind as he suckled on her lips, feeling her heaving body in his arms. He didn't want her to accept his kisses because she was afraid to refuse.

He wanted her to want him.

"Do ye want me tae stop?" he asked huskily.

Rora was barely coherent. "If…if ye want tae."

He grasped her by the chin, his face very close to hers as he stared into her eyes. "Nay," he muttered. "Listen tae me. Do *ye* want me tae stop?

It seemed to occur to her what he was asking. Her mouth worked a moment as she tried to come up with the correct words. "Ye should," she breathed. "If Miss Lizelle were tae know…."

She trailed off and he understood, at least from her perspective. If Lizelle discovered he'd kissed Rora, then it would go very badly for her. He simply sat there a moment, gazing down at her, into that sweet face with those glorious eyes. He was drawn to those eyes time and time again. The hand on her chin began to caress her skin.

"Has anyone ever done this to ye, Rora?" he asked softly. "Have ye never been kissed?"

She shook her head, quivering as his hand move to the soft skin of her neck. "N-Never."

"No man has forced himself upon ye?"

She was quiet for a moment. "Some of Laird Robert's men have tried," she said. "When I tell Miss Lizelle, she becomes very angry and Laird Robert dismisses them."

"So no man has… touched ye?"

She shook her head. "Nay, m'laird."

He gave her a half-grin. "Considerin' that I just kissed ye, addressin' me formally sounds strange."

"Then… then what should I call ye?"

He leaned forward, capturing her sweet lips in his. He suckled her bottom lip before releasing it. "My name is Jackston," he whispered. "Let me hear ye say it."

Rora was breathing so heavily it sounded like she was gasping. "Jackston."

He licked her upper lip. "Say it again."

"*Jackston.*"

Grinning, his mouth slanted over hers again, pulling her so tightly against him that she grunted with the force of it. She was sweet and soft, warm and pliable, and his mouth soon left hers to force a blazing trail down her neck and to her shoulder, where tender white skin beckoned. He suckled gently on her skin, pulling the top of her tunic away and down one arm, pulling it so low that he exposed her left breast.

Jackston could feel Rora tense in his arms as her breast sprang free and she tried to cover it back up, but he wouldn't allow it. He trapped her arm with a big hand as his mouth moved down her shoulder to the swell of her breast. She was starting to gasp now, in both uncertainty and in passion, and when his heated mouth claimed a nipple, her gasps became louder.

God, those sounds fueled his lust!

But he didn't want their passion to be heard. In order to quickly silence her, Jackston's mouth quickly returned to hers, kissing her deeply to stifle her noise even as a hand moved to her exposed breast and fondled her. He pulled at her nipple, teasing it, feeling her buck and quiver in his arms. Nothing in his life had ever excited him so much and his stiff manhood was straining against his *braies*. More kissing, more fondling, and he was ready to push her onto her back and throw up her skirts.

But something stopped him.

Attracted as he was to her, he simply couldn't bring himself to take her in a stable, grinding her tender back into the urine-soaked earth. He had more respect for her than that and, no matter how physically ready he was to mate with her, he just couldn't do it.

More than that, there was something emotional between them now, a warmth and a bond like he'd never experienced. But she was a servant... God help him, she was a servant and his parents would never accept her as a wife to their heroic son, a man who would assume the Daviot lordship someday as the 2nd Lord Daviot, heir to a small empire. A woman sold into servitude as the wife of a great warrior?

It could not exist in his world.

More thoughts of taking her to England swamped him and his lusty kisses eased. Confusion was sucking the passion right out of him and he slowed his onslaught, pulling back to look at the woman as she lay dazed in his arms. The truth was that even if he took her to England to start a life with her, his parents would still know the truth. They would know he'd taken a servant for his bride and they would be shamed by it. Their foolish son would have passed on wealthy Lizelle Menzies only to marry a servant girl by the name of Rora of Lonmay.

He had to stop and think about all of this. But one thing was for certain; he knew he couldn't leave Rora behind.

Wouldn't leave her behind.

But he couldn't seem to let her go at the moment, either, and that indiscretion was his undoing. As he went back to suckling gently on Rora's naked breast, one of Lizelle's women, a round little mouse who spied and shared gossip with her mistress, made her way into the barn. The woman had kept her eye on Rora. She had seen from her vantage point in Lizelle's bower window when the servant girl had fled the manse and disappeared into the stables.

Suspicious and nosy, the woman had quickly followed simply to see what Rora was up to and having no idea that Jackston was in the stable, too. But when she peered around the side of the entry and saw Rora in the arms of Miss Lizelle's betrothed, she nearly shrieked aloud. She saw the man nursing on Rora's naked breasts, the servant girl with her arms over her head, letting him take advantage of her. It was both shocking and disgusting.

Miss Lizelle must know!

In a flash, the round little woman was scurrying for the manse with a great tale to tell.

Chapter Four

That evening

AFTER FINALLY PERMITTING RORA TO go back to her duties because she was fearful that their tryst would be discovered, Jackston lingered with his horse a little longer, not wanting to retreat into the manse and back into the lair where a spinster sister was pinching him and Lizelle was trying to show him such domestic bliss. He was quite certain Lizelle had changed out of her stained clothing by now and was waiting for him to come to her and, frankly, he was surprised that she hadn't come looking for him. But he was grateful for small mercies. His time in the stable had allowed him to come to know Rora in a most intimate way and he was more convinced than ever that he was smitten with her. Perhaps even more than smitten.

But that was something he had to sort out for himself.

So, he remained with his horse, pondering the dilemma he was facing. He'd been reluctant to come to Braelaw before he ever met Rora, and she was most certainly something he hadn't expected. He began to wonder if his attraction to her was some extreme reaction to his unwillingness to marry Lizelle, but he'd never been the type to fall for a woman, at least not to the point where he was thinking of marrying her.

God's Bones… what was he going to do?

Eventually, the sun began to set in the west, casting long shadows in the stables and the grooms entered with covered fish oil lamps to feed the beasts their evening meal. When the grooms entered, Jackston exited into the stable yard and headed to the manse beyond. The wall surrounding the manse was sealed off, the gates closed as the business for the day had been finished and people were finishing up their tasks before the evening meal commenced. Jackston could smell roasting meat on the breeze and it was making him hungry. Fortifying himself with a deep breath for courage, he headed into the manse.

Robert was near the door in conversation with his majordomo when he entered and Jackston was once again subjected to the man's very warm reception. But the moment he set foot inside the manse, Jackston took on the look of the hunted. He knew there were at least two hungry females nearby and he wanted to be ready when he was set upon.

Oblivious to Jackston's hunt-or-be-hunted demeanor, Robert led him into the great hall, which now had people in it, mostly senior soldiers, and other people that Jackston didn't know about – or even care about. In fact, he was thinking of a plan to get Robert alone so he could relay his decision to the man when his host indicated for him to sit at the head of the table.

In the host's spot.

Jackston groaned inwardly; Robert wasn't making this simple for him in the least but perhaps that was the man's plan. Perhaps Robert knew what Jackston was thinking, returning to Lizelle after all of these years, and he was showing him what it would be like when Jackston, in fact, was the lord of Braelaw. Much as Lizelle had done, Robert was creating quite the domestic picture – a prosperous home, many servants, and soldiers at his disposal. Any man would be proud and happy to have such a thing.

But not Jackston; it was starting to make him sick.

"Greetings, m'laird."

An unfamiliar voice sounded in his ear and Jackston turned to see the spinster sister planting herself next to him, her round face ripe with delight. Her head was severely wimpled with scarlet fabric, blending into scarlet robes, and with her rosy cheeks, Jackston couldn't help but think she looked much like a beet. She winked at him and giggled. He rolled his eyes and looked away.

Truth be told, he didn't have any patience with the woman whatsoever. He'd reached his limit and was finished feeling the need to be polite. The entire French army couldn't intimidate him, but he realized he'd permitted the entire Menzies family to intimidate him to a certain extent. Since when did a man not speak his mind? Since when did *he* not speak his mind? When a servant offered him wine, he not only took the cup but also the pitcher the woman was holding. He drank his entire cup of wine in two big gulps and poured himself another. He was about to take another drink when he felt the spinster sister's hand on his thigh. Reaching under the table, he grabbed her hand and squeezed it so hard that he nearly snapped her fingers.

The spinster sister screamed and yanked her hand away, looking at Jackston as if he'd done something terrible to her. He met her gaze steadily.

"You willna touch me," he growled. "I've had enough of yer pinchin' and yer advances. Do it again and I'll break yer hand. Is this in any way unclear?"

The woman turned positively ashen. Holding her aching fingers, she stumbled up from the bench and scampered off, straight to Robert, who was on the opposite side of the table speaking with one of his men. Jackston watched as the sister began crying to Robert, pointing to Jackston at the other end of the table, and he clearly saw Robert's reaction. The man shoved his sister aside and evidently told her to leave the hall, which she did, in tears. Jackston braced himself as Robert drew near.

"Is there a problem, Jackston?" he asked, seemingly concerned. "My sister said that she has offended ye."

Jackston smirked; he couldn't help it. "Is that what she said? Yer sister has made unwanted advances tae me since I came tae Braelaw. If she wasna rubbin' her feet on me leg, then she was pinchin' me thigh. I willna stand for it any longer."

Robert looked stricken. "God's Blood," he hissed. "Please accept me apologies, Jackston. I had no idea."

Jackston was in an increasingly foul mood. "Keep yer sister in check, Menzies. The next man might not be as patient with her as I was."

Robert looked as if he'd been physically struck; he literally took a step back, shocked with the venom coming forth from Jackston. But in that reaction, Jackston suddenly saw his way out of all of this – perhaps if he was nasty enough and mean enough, Robert would cancel the marriage contract himself. Since Jackston was expected to sit through this meal, anyway, why not make it a meal to remember? Truthfully, perhaps that had been the answer all along. It wasn't Lizelle had had to discourage.

It was Robert.

He was willing to try anything at this point.

"Again, me apologies," Robert said stiffly, both contrite and offended by Jackston's attitude. "I will make sure she doesna join us again."

"Keep her away from me."

"I said I would."

Jackston's gaze lingered on Robert, bordering on hostile, before turning away to down his second cup of wine in three swallows. More wine was poured. By this time, more people were entering the hall, including Lizelle. Before her father could warn her off of Jackston's foul mood, she rushed straight to the end of the table and right into Jackston's orbit.

"Jackston," she greeted, looking a bit flushed in her pale yellow brocade. "I am so glad ye dinna leave!"

Jackston looked at her over the rim of his cup. "I told ye I wouldna."

"But ye dinna come back to me chamber."

Jackston looked away. "I have seen enough of yer chamber," he said. "Sit down if ye have a mind tae. Dunna stand there. It makes me nervous."

Lizelle quickly obeyed. She planted herself in the seat vacated by her aunt, eyeing Jackston most curiously. He seemed to be… unhappy. There was no hint of warmth on his face. Lizelle caught a glimpse of her father and, noting the man's concerned features, she thought that something might have been amiss but she didn't dare ask what it might be. In her mind, perhaps Jackston was unhappy for a reason.

Perhaps it was a guilty conscience.

Aye, she'd been told by her woman what Jackston had been up to in the stable when she had been changing into a clean dress. *Suckling on Rora*, she'd been told. That silly little twit who had spilled all over her had evidently done it on purpose so she could rid herself of Lizelle and seduce her betrothed. At least, that was the general consensus among Lizelle and her women.

At first, Lizelle had been crushed. Genuinely crushed. But after the tears of anger and embarrassment faded, she was certain that Rora had instigated the entire thing. Men were weak to feminine charms, after all, and surely Rora, who had run from every other man who'd ever tried to seduce her, must have finally found that part of her that lusted after a handsome man. She'd turned those charms loose on Jackston, who had been unable to resist.

Sickened. Lizelle genuinely felt sickened by it. But she'd had time to think, to calm herself, and to understand that Jackston could do whatever he wanted. He was a man, after all, and it was not up to her to judge his actions. As long as he married her, Lizelle would look the other way if he had an occasional dalliance with a servant. Her mother did that a great deal with her father, so it was the example that Lizelle had set for her. Men philandered, women ignored.

Therefore, Lizelle would not mention what she knew. She would not confront him. She *had* to marry the man no matter what the circumstances. She didn't even care that she was sacrificing her self-respect to do it.

But her attitude towards Rora was markedly different.

She hadn't seen the servant girl since the woman had been thrown from her chamber. Rora's tasks were usually limited to serving food and helping with the bath. When she wasn't doing those things, she was working in the kitchens, especially in the evenings. Therefore, Lizelle had been given all afternoon to plan her punishment for Rora. That hidden heart that Rora had spoken of, the one of fear and cruelty, was about to be revealed.

So Lizelle would bide her time.

As she sat there and thought of clever conversations to start with Jackston, more people entered the room. Some of these people were neighbors, having received a missive that afternoon that Lizelle's betrothed had arrived. So, in a sense, this was a celebration. She wasn't sure if her father had told Jackston that the evening meal would be anything but a quiet sup, but she suspected he hadn't. Nothing like announcing a betrothal in front of a room full of people so that the groom couldn't gracefully bow out of it.

Lizelle's lyre player found himself a warm corner of the room and, even now, faint lyre music floated over the throng of people as they found their places at the tables and more wine was brought forth. Jackston was on his fourth cup of wine now, feeling the fortification of it pulsing through his veins and thinking that the last thing he wanted to hear was that ridiculous lyre. At least Lizelle had kept her mouth shut and he didn't have to listen to her foolish chatter, but he was seriously coming to wonder who all of these people were. Robert was greeting them all quite graciously as his majordomo found them seating in the hall that was growing increasingly crowded. When an older couple, well-dressed, were finally seated at one of the two big feasting tables, Robert finally raised his voice.

"Me friends," he said, beaming, "it is good tae see all of ye here tonight. It is a special occasion, it 'tis, and I wanted ye all tae share it with us. I know it was short notice tae ask ye tae feast with us on this night, but we were rather surprised by our guest of honor's visit today. It is, therefore, with great pride that I introduce ye tae me daughter's betrothed, Sir Jackston Forbes. Let us greet him properly."

Everyone gasped and clapped, cheering as Jackston sat there, dumbfounded. Lizelle stood up next to him, beaming from ear to ear, clapping her hands and pointing him out as he continued to sit there. Like a bump on a log, his father would have said. As much as Jackston didn't want any part of whatever this feast was turning out to be, he knew some of these people surely knew his parents and, even if he didn't care about embarrassing himself, he didn't want to shame them. Begrudgingly, he set his wine down and stood up, looking uncomfortable as the crowded cheered him. At the other end of the hall, Robert was cheering the loudest.

"I'm sure ye've all heard of Jackston," he said. "One of our own who made a name for himself at the great battle of Crécy two years ago when the French king was defeated. We are very proud tae know Jackston and I know me own daughter would like tae say somethin'. Lizzie?"

Jackston didn't really think this could get any worse. He was floored by the fact that there had evidently been a feast set up in his honor and he hadn't even known about it. That was probably a good thing because he wouldn't have been happy about it had he known; at least this way, he couldn't back out. He was trapped. As he rubbed his eyes, feeling the alcohol swim in his head, Lizelle spoke.

"As ye have probably suspected, Jackie knew nothin' about this celebration," she said, laughing as a room full of people laughed. "It was me da's idea when Jackie arrived today and I thought it would be wonderful. I think... I think we have much tae be grateful for. Jackie and I knew each other as wee bairns and, many a time, he would save me from monsters or black knights. We played many games as children and that was when I came tae know and love him. He was only a lad when he vowed tae marry me and tae see him here this night, returned tae me as he said he would, shows what a great man of honor he is. Most men would have forgotten such a pledge but Jackie dinna."

She was looking at Jackston as she spoke, adoringly, and he simply looked at her as if he held nothing but contempt. He couldn't believe he'd been caged up like this, praise heaped upon him, being pushed more and more into something he didn't want to do.

God's Bones, he'd had so many plans to get out of this betrothal – of trying to manipulate Lizelle into backing out of it, of trying to be nasty enough that perhaps Robert wouldn't want his daughter to marry such a man, but none of it had worked. Then he got the bright idea to simply speak with Robert and tell him that he could not marry Lizelle, but how could he do that now? Now, all of these people – people who surely knew his parents – knew of the betrothal. Was it actually possible that he wasn't going to be able to get out of this? That he would be saddled with Lizelle for the rest of his life? A huge part of him refused to believe that. He *wouldn't* be pushed into this. But that part of him, so loyal to his parents, was having second doubts.

… was he really trapped?

Thankfully, the food started coming forth, with several servants bringing out great dishes in a serious display of wealth, and everyone was distracted. He was no longer the center of attention. Roast swan, peacock, and fowl were brought out, birds that had been cooked and then their feathers reattached in a somewhat morbid display. At least, Jackston always thought it was morbid. Bowls of warmed rose water for diners to wash their hands in were brought out along with more food – boiled vegetables, pies, and potages.

Male servants lugged in big wheels of cheese for the diners to cut their own portions from. And bread – huge amounts of bread were brought out. As people began to focus on the food, the lyre player began to strum. It took Jackston a moment to realize the lyre player was now standing between him and Lizelle, strumming loudly. When he began to sing, Jackston nearly punched him in the mouth.

> *Divine Lovers!*
> *Whom God has brought together!*
> *Such love only grows,*
> *Delightful...*
> *Delicious...*
> *Such love will never die!*
> *Ah! Divine Lovers, rejoice!*

Jackston turned away from the lyre player and sucked down about half of his wine. As the lyre player continued to strum and sing another chorus, he could feel someone tugging on his sleeve.

"That song was written for us," Lizelle said over the lyre player's strumming. "My minstrel wrote it in yer honor. Is it not beautiful?"

At that point, Jackston wasn't sure what he could even say. The whole situation was like a nightmare with no end. He hated every bit of it but it was his own fault that he'd been unwilling to speak up until now, unwilling to hurt feelings or damage honor. Now, he was trapped in a quagmire of his own doing. Therefore, he simply shrugged to her question and took another drink of wine, the only thing giving him comfort at the moment.

But the situation soon changed.

Rora appeared, entering the hall from a servant's entrance and bearing two big trenchers. She slipped up behind Jackston and Lizelle, carefully placing a trencher in front of Lizelle before serving Jackston. In fact, Jackston didn't even see her until she placed the trencher in front of Lizelle but as she set his down, a very heavy trencher bearing a good deal of food on it, Lizelle gasped.

"Rora!" she hissed. "Ye should have served Jackston first! He is our guest!"

Rora looked at Lizelle in confusion, mostly because Lizelle had made it very clear, always, that she was the first one to be served regardless of who was sitting at the table. In fact, at meals, it was Rora's sole duty to serve Lizelle. But she quickly submitted, having been taught long ago never to argue with her mistress.

"I am sorry, miss," she said. "I will remember for the next time."

Jackston was looking at Lizelle over the rim of his cup. "She served ye because ye are her mistress," he said. "I am sure that is what ye've taught her."

Lizelle began to turn red again, seeing that Jackston was once again defending her servant. *A woman he suckled on!* It was difficult not to feel a good deal of shame at that moment, being rebuked in front of a woman who had seduced her betrothed. She looked at Jackston, wondering why he didn't want to suckle on her the way he's suckled on Rora. Hurt and fury began to fill her.

"She knows tae serve guests first," she said steadily, eyeing Rora and feeling an unnatural amount of hatred for the woman. "Jackston's food is not steamin' hot, Rora. Bring him hot food."

Rora didn't even hesitate; she picked up Jackston's heavy trencher, which was still hot but not steaming as Lizelle had pointed out. She moved so quickly that Jackston couldn't even stop her; she was running from the hall before he could take another breath. He watched her go a moment before turning his attention to Lizelle.

"That wasna necessary," he said in a low voice. "The food was hot enough."

Lizelle smiled thinly. "I want tae ensure everythin' is perfect for ye," she said. Then, she suddenly stood up. "In fact, I will make sure of it. Will ye please excuse me?"

She was gone before Jackston could say a word, rushing after Rora and back towards the kitchens. Jackston watched her until she disappeared from the hall, thinking that it probably wasn't a good idea for Lizelle to run after Rora like that. Knowing the hostility Lizelle had towards Rora, surely it couldn't be a good thing to allow the woman unsupervised time with her, but the truth was that he couldn't stop it. He couldn't even go after her. It would look suspicious if he did.

So, he sat there and worried, wondering what was going on out of his line of sight. After his fourth cup of wine, his head was seriously starting to swim so he pushed it aside in favor of boiled water that had been flavored with smashed pomegranate seeds and sprigs of mint. If he had much more of the wine, he was afraid he might say or do something wildly offensive, so it was better not to press his luck. In a volatile situation as he was, he didn't need much to push him over the edge.

The minutes seemed to drag by as he waited for Lizelle to return. Robert tried to motion him down to his end of the table, but Jackston pretended he didn't see the man waving him over. He had no intention of being sociable this night. More minutes passed and he was growing increasingly nervous until Lizelle suddenly reappeared and reclaimed her seat beside him.

Jackston looked closely at the woman. She seemed rather flustered, pink-cheeked, and, before he could really see what it was, she wiped something off of her right cheek. It looked like a speck of something. It was red, or so he thought.

… oh, God… could it be blood?

"Not to worry, Jackie," Lizelle said, seemingly out of breath. "Yer food should be here shortly."

He peered at her intently. "Where did ye go?"

Lizelle wouldn't look at him. She picked up her spoon and began pushing the food around on her trencher. "I told ye," she said. "I must always make sure yer food is prepared well. It should be here shortly."

He didn't believe her. Nor did he trust her. Something about her manner had him quite wary of what had happened in those minutes she was gone. As he eyed the woman, wondering if he really did see her wipe blood from her cheek, Rora suddenly came up behind him again, placing a trencher of steaming food in front of him.

Jackston saw the food and Rora's hand but by the time he turned to thank her, she had already turned away from him. The first thing that struck him was her hair; that beautiful blonde hair wasn't neat like he'd seen all day; it was askew. She wasn't even wearing her kerchief. In fact, her hair was in her face and he reached out to grab her arm before she could get away. She resisted, slightly, trying to pull away, and that was when he caught sight of her face.

His heart sank.

Rora's lip was cut and there was blood around her nose. The left side of her face was already bruising and he could see that her left eye was swelling. Someone had beaten the woman and he had a fairly good idea who it was. As Rora continued to try and pull away, Jackston shifted his grip and latched on to her arm. It was a viselike grip and there was no chance for her to pull free. Her struggles ceased but she wouldn't look at him. Jackston took a look at the damage on her face and sighed heavily.

"Who did this to ye?" he asked quietly.

Beside him, Lizelle turned to look at Rora as if only just noticing her. "She is clumsy," she said, answering for Roar. "She fell in the kitchen. I saw her."

Jackston never took his eyes off of Rora's face. He felt so much rage and disgust at that moment that it was difficult to contain it. That beautiful, sweet woman had been beaten within an inch of her life for what – food that wasn't hot enough? Somehow, Jackston suspected it was more than that. Something told him that there was far more to this than a simple beating. He looked at Lizelle.

"Ye did this tae her," he rumbled. "Why?"

Lizelle wouldn't look at him; she seemed more interested in her food. "'Household matters shouldna concern ye," she said. "I do as I must tae discipline me servants. Her face will heal."

He stared at her. *She knows*, he thought. He didn't know how Lizelle knew he'd shown attention to Rora, or possibly she even knew about the kiss, but his instincts were telling him that Rora's life was in danger now. If he left Braelaw without her, then something terrible was going to happen to her.

He could feel it in his bones.

"I asked ye a question," he said to Lizelle. "Why did ye beat her?"

Lizelle spooned boiled peas into her mouth. "And I told ye it shouldna concern ye. She's *me* servant."

She was being deliberately evasive and Jackston knew, at that moment, that he had to make a decision. He could continue to allow this charade to continue, to allow Robert and Lizelle to believe that he was going to follow through on his vow of marriage, or he could take a stand. If he didn't, then he would be a weak example of a man, indeed. This was no longer about his parents' honor or even his own honor. Now, this was about doing the right and decent thing. All thoughts of Rora aside, he would never marry someone like Lizelle, for her hidden heart was a dark thing, indeed.

Now, it was time for him to show his hidden heart.

And it was about to roar.

Without another word, he stood up and kept his firm grip on Rora's arm. She was resisting him, fearful, but he was gentle as he pulled her away from the table and into the center of the hall, exactly between the two tables. He had something to say and everyone was going to hear it. He was about to deny this betrothal and he wanted to make sure everyone understood why.

Especially Rora.

He cleared his throat loudly and held up a hand to gain everyone's attention. When all eyes turned to him, he felt his courage surge. "I have somethin' tae say," he said as the room quieted down abruptly. Pulling Rora in front of him, he forced her to lift her head as he pulled her hair back. "Can everyone see this? Can everyone see the lass' face?"

He displayed Rora in a circle, making sure everyone could see her split lip and bruised face. He could hear people gasping and whispering. It was a terrible sight and a confusing one. No one was really sure what was going on, especially Lizelle, who had a look of horror about her. But when everyone had a chance to see Rora, Jackston focused on Robert.

"Yer daughter did this," he said, listening to gasps of shock flitter throughout the room. "She beat this poor lass bloody because the woman served me a trencher of food that wasna hot enough. At least, Lizelle dinna think so. Robert, do ye truly allow yer daughter tae beat her servants like this? Because it is a shameful thing, indeed, if ye do."

Robert's eyes bugged as he struggled for a reply. But Jackston wasn't going to permit it. He held up a hand to silence the man as Rora, standing next to him, hung her head and began to weep softly.

"I dunna care if ye know or not," Jackston said to the man. "I came here today because me da forced me. As a lad, I made a promise tae Lizelle tae marry her. I was twelve at the time; I dinna know any better. I thought that I would want tae marry her someday. But I was wrong... so very wrong. That lad ye knew has grown up and become a man. A man who has seen the world and knows somethin' of it. I came today tae tell ye that I wouldna be marryin' yer daughter, but the moment I came through the gates, ye showered me with praise and wine, so much so that I never had a chance tae tell ye why I'd really come. And then yer daughter forced me tae sit with her, with her ladies present, and all the while that ridiculous musician played music overhead. Did ye not stop tae think that, mayhap, I had somethin' tae say about all of this? Did ye ever stop tae think that ye were holdin' a man tae a lad's vow? Ye and yer daughter were ready tae push me intae this marriage no matter how I felt."

Robert's shocked expression had morphed into one of guilt and sadness. He scratched his head, nervously, so very embarrassed in front of all of his guests. "We… we were happy tae have ye here, Jackston," he said quietly. "'Tis not a crime tae welcome ye as we did."

Jackston shook his head. "Nay, it 'twas not a crime," he agreed. "But this feast – ye invited everyone and announced the betrothal without even speakin' tae me about it. Did ye even think tae ask me what I thought? How I felt? Or do ye still let yer spoilt daughter push ye around as she always did? She did it as a child and she continues tae do it now, Robert. When are ye tae be a man and stand up tae her?"

Robert held Jackston's stare steadily for a moment before sinking down into his seat. All of what Jackston had said was true. In fact, nearly everyone in that room knew it. They all knew Lizelle and how vicious she was, and how Robert simply looked the other way. In fact, most of the people were becoming sympathetic with Jackston as they came to understand the gist of the situation. It was a shameful thing, indeed.

"What would ye have me say, Jackston?" Robert finally asked, his voice trembling. "I dunna know what ye want me tae say."

Jackston was beyond feeling pity for the man; he just couldn't bring himself to feel anything at all.

"Say nothin'," he said, "because right now, I'm doin' the talkin'. 'Tis the first time ye've let me speak since I arrived. Now, if I had come and Lizelle had grown out of her spoilt ways, mayhap things would have been different. But she is not only spoilt, she has also become wicked. Instead of a grown woman with a kind heart, I find a vicious, nasty woman who beats on her servants. I canna and willna sully the Forbes name with a wife like that. In me world, honor and compassion and a good heart mean more to me than the wealth of the Menzies' name. I would have told ye all of this privately, but ye never gave me the chance. And when Lizelle decided tae beat this poor woman tonight, it was the final act as far as I'm concerned. I can no longer remain silent."

Robert simply nodded his head, sadly, but Lizelle stood up from her seat, her entire face red with shame and anger. She had been listening to Jackston's speech with horror and outrage to the point where she felt the need to defend herself. She had to deflect some of that shame.

"Ye dallied with me servant today!" she accused. "Me woman saw ye with her in the stable. For the fact that she seduced me betrothed, I am in me right tae punish her!"

Jackston shook his head. Lizelle would never even know what he was talking about when he spoke of good hearts. She had been a spoilt child and she was a spoilt woman, unable to understand what it meant to be decent and true.

"I was never yer betrothed, Lizelle," he said, almost sadly. "Ye took a lad's promise and tried tae hold me tae it. Ye tried tae force it down me throat without even askin' me. I've outgrown ye, lass."

Lizelle was losing something she very badly wanted. She wasn't an affable loser; she never had been. All of her anger was turning in Rora's direction now as her betrothal was slipping through her fingers.

"So ye've outgrown me," she hissed. "But ye're not so grown up that ye still find a servant lass appealin' like the buck that ye are. Ye speak of a good heart but ye've dirtied yerself by seducin' me maid. And now ye use it as an excuse tae break our betrothal? Ye're a fool, Jackston Forbes, and I want nothin' tae do with ye. Get out of me sight. I never want tae see ye again!"

It was Lizelle's way of saving her pride. Jackston understood that. In fact, he was coming to understand a lot about her and he thanked God that he'd had the courage to stand up to her and her father before the situation grew out of hand. Still, he had to admit that this was all a little sad – sad for Robert, for Rora, and even Lizelle, to a certain point. She was his childhood friend and all she wanted was to be married.

But it wasn't going to be to him.

"I learned somethin' today," he said after a moment. "Someone told me that we all have hidden hearts. Lizelle, yers is dark. I will pray that someday it comes intae the light. Robert, yer hidden heart is yer fear of yer daughter and of the continuation of yer family. I understand that. But me hidden heart… I suppose in a world where honor and reputation mean everythin', I've discovered that mine is softer than I thought it was. Mayhap it wants tae find happiness, even if that happiness is with someone… unexpected."

He was looking at Rora as he spoke. She was still looking at her feet, with tears streaming down her battered cheeks. But as he spoke that last word – *unexpected* – he squeezed her arm gently and she lifted her eyes, looking at him. He smiled into that beaten, bloodied face and, from the look in her eyes, Jackston knew that she was aware of who he meant.

Her.

There was nothing more to say at that point. Without another word, not even to Robert, Jackston left the great hall and pulled Rora with him out into the night beyond. It was a brilliant night, clear and cold. But to Jackston and Rora, it was the most beautiful night imaginable, the beginning of a life together that neither one of them could have ever imagined.

As they traveled the quiet miles back to Blackbog Castle on that cold and gentle night, it didn't seem to matter to Jackston that he was going to have to explain to his parents that he'd broken his vow with Lizelle. Somehow, he knew when he explained things to them, that they would understand. Truth be told, they would probably be glad.

And they would learn to love Rora just as he did.

For the Highlander and the servant lass, a chance encounter with forbidden love became a great story of hope and devotion. Having returned to Dunster Castle as Jackston had planned, the English knew Lady Rora Forbes as a gentle, humorous, and brilliant woman that her Scots husband was very much in love with. No one ever knew Rora's humble beginnings or the lengths Jackston had gone through to marry her. For in truth, there was nothing about Rora that was different from any other noble woman.

A woman with a beautiful heart, hidden no more.

Epilogue

1368 A.D.
Dunster Castle

RORA HAD BEEN watching the situation for quite some time.

It was a difficult situation for all concerned; word had come from Blackbog Castle that Alexander Forbes had passed away after a brief illness last winter and Jackston's mother was begging her son to return home to assume his rightful place. But Jackston was torn – he'd been living in England for over half his life and returning to Scotland, although it had always been in the back of his mind, wasn't something he was ready to do. He'd all but adopted England as his home.

So, Rora watched her husband as he paced the battlements, sometimes in quiet discussion with his eldest son, Donnan, who served with his father, or sometimes with his cousin who was the Lord of Dunster. Somewhere back in the family lines, a Forbes ancestor had married in to the House of de Moyon, the Lords of Dunster, and now it was the House of Forbes who ruled over these wild and forbidden lands near the Exmoor forest. Jackston had served his cousin for years as the man's counsel and most powerful warrior, but with that message from Scotland, it was all about to come to an end.

Twenty years of marriage and eight children later, Rora knew her husband's heart even more than he did. Seated in the solar of Dunster, she could see the man through the lancet window. That was how she'd been able to watch him for most of the morning, at least when he came into her line of sight. But he'd been all over the place that morning, pacing, thinking, and trying to determine the course of the further for him and for his family. But, in truth, where was nothing more to think about. As far as Rora was concerned, the path had been set.

She suspected that Jackston knew that, too.

At her feet sat three of their eight children, all three of them girls. But the first five had been boys, now either fostering or at Dunster serving their father and cousin. But the little girls were her band of angels, as their father called them, and even now they sat on the floor of Dunster's solar, sewing little squares of fabric their mother had given them on their way to making a coverlet.

Even at their ages – Amelia was seven years of age, Cora was five years of age, and little Eleanor was three years of age – they were diligent in their work. That came from their mother, who even after these years still had the heart of a hard worker and a good servant. She was involved in every aspect of Dunster, including the kitchens, and it made the Lady of Dunster's life considerably easier. Jackston had given up long ago chiding her on involving herself in the menial work around the castle; she enjoyed it, and it was ingrained into her, so he didn't have the heart to scold her about it. If it made her happy, then he was happy.

But the result with his leniency of her was very industrious children. Rora had taught them all to work hard, even the boys before they went away to foster. Jackston had eight children who weren't afraid to cut wood or sweep a floor, something that, in truth, he was very proud of. He and Rora had productive children.

But they were all English-born and bred.

That was a good deal of his problem, Rora knew. Even though she and Jackston were born in the highlands, their children weren't. That had been the core of Jackston's turmoil but when Eleanor pricked her finger with the bone needle and began to wail, Rora pushed aside thoughts of her overwrought husband to tend to her weeping child. It was just a tiny prick, but Eleanor wept as though the needle had gone straight through her finger. As Rora was dabbing away the blood and kissing the wound, Jackston suddenly appeared in the doorway.

"What have ye done to me bairn?" he demanded, though he was jesting. He swooped in and picked up Eleanor, kissing the injured finger she shoved into his face. "Ellie, lass, 'twill be fine. 'Tis just a little mark."

Eleanor was convinced it was a much larger wound even as her father soothed her. Rora watched her husband as he tenderly soothed the toddler.

"As ye can see, I've been stickin' needles in her," Rora said. "'Tis a good thing ye came tae save her when ye did."

Jackston kissed the little finger one last time and rocked the baby, who was calming in her father's loving presence. "'Tis fortunate she has me tae save her from her terrible mother," he said, noticing that the other two girls were sewing diligently. "Ah, now – are ye makin' something fine for me?"

Amelia, the eldest, nodded firmly, her auburn curls bouncing. "Aye, Papa. We are making a coverlet for your bed!"

She sounded very proud and Jackston grinned. "Ye're angels, indeed, and a fine tribute tae yer mother."

"I thought ye said I was a terrible mother," Rora said.

Jackston snorted. "A slip of me tongue."

Rora grinned as she shook her head as she threaded her own needle. "Careful with yer tongue," she said. "Men have been known tae lose theirs for lesser insults."

Jackston was still grinning when she glanced up at him. "I adore ye, lass, and ye know it."

"Now ye try tae make amends, do ye?"

Jackston laughed softly and put Eleanor to her feet when she squired. "What can I do tae make it up tae ye?"

"Ye can tell me what ye're thinkin'. I've been watchin' ye pace all morning, Jackie. What are ye thinkin'?"

Jackston sobered dramatically. Heaving a sigh, he lowered his gaze and began his pacing again, only on a smaller scale. The solar wasn't big enough for him to really gain any steam in, so he simply shuffled around until he came to the hearth. Then, he leaned on it, gazing into the low-burning flames.

"I'm thinkin' many things," he muttered. "Too many things."

"Like what?"

"Guilt. I havena seen me da in four years. He died without seein' me before he passed."

"That couldna be helped."

He sighed again. "I know," he said. "But I feel guilty that I wasna there. All he had is Blackbog Castle and the lands it sits upon. Now it's just me mum…."

"Lilliana is a strong woman. She'll do what needs tae be done now that yer da is gone."

Jackston nodded but he was becoming agitated. "I know she's strong," he said. "But she shouldna have tae be strong. I should be there."

"So ye want tae go?"

He shook his head. "Nay," he said. "That is the problem. I dunna want tae go home. England is me home; *our* home. Dunster is our home. It's where our children were born. And our children, Rora – they're English. Only the older boys have been tae Blackbog and the highlands, but all of them are English tae the bone. We canna take a brood of English bairns intae the highlands. They would be outlanders. It wouldna be fair tae them."

He had a point. Rora had been thinking the same thing but she didn't want to voice her concerns. This was Jackston's decision and she knew he was torn over it. It wasn't that he didn't love the land of his birth; it was simply he loved England better. Jackston was a man of the world.

"What choice have ye, then?" she asked as she continued to sew. "Did ye speak with Ramsey?"

Ramsey Forbes was the Lord of Dunster. Jackston nodded his head. "He doesna want tae lose me, but he will abide by my decision."

"And Donnie? I saw ye speaking with him, too."

Jackston lifted his eyebrows at the mention of his nineteen-year-old son. Donnan Forbes was a shining star of a young man, verging on becoming a fully-fledged knight. He'd fostered at Lioncross Abbey Castle as well as Kirk Castle on the marches. He was a strong fighter and a brilliant tactician, and Jackston was immensely proud of the lad. He had four other sons – Rory, James, Gregor, and Finlay – and the boys were strong, proud, and intelligent. But There was something about Donnan that set him apart from the rest. Perhaps it was because he was Jackston's first born. Whatever it was, father and son were quite close. Jackston trusted Donnan's opinions.

"Donnie," he muttered, clearly mulling over the conversation he'd had with his eldest. "Donnie is concerned with tradition. He's concerned what will happen if I dunna take me da's place at Blackbog."

"If we do not take our rightful place at Blackbog Castle, the clans will absorb it and it will be no more."

The voice came from the doorway. Rora and Jackston looked over to see Donnan standing there, stepping in to the room. He was taller than his father though not as bulky, with the same long flowing auburn hair. Donnan Forbes looked to his mother.

"That is what I told him," he said, pointing to his father. "I am afraid that if Papa does not go to the highlands to take his rightful place, then Blackbog and the history of the Forbes of Blackbog will be no more."

Rora nodded faintly. "That is true," she said. "But ye know yer father doesna feel the heart of the highlands. He was born there but his soul doesna breathe that air. He is more at home in England, here at Dunster. But he's Scots by birth and that makes him torn."

Donnan nodded. "I realize that," he said, "but a legacy is too precious to be given up so easily."

"Yer da understands that."

Donnan glanced at his father. "I have been thinking on the problem and I believe I have come up with a solution."

Jackston liked the sound of that. "Speak, Donnie lad."

Now Donnan fixed his father in the eye. "I think I should go."

Jackston couldn't conceal his surprise at that suggestions. "But why?" he asked. "Ye were born here, at Dunster. Ye've fostered in the finest houses. Why would ye go tae the highlands when that isn'a the life ye've known?"

Donnan took a few more steps in to the chamber, thoughtfully, squatting down beside his baby sister when she toddled over to him. He put his arms around her and hugged her.

"Because I have fostered in the finest houses," he said quietly. "I have known all of the advantages you could give me. I have been well-schooled and I understand our lands and the politics. But I have more ambition simply to be a knight to a great lord, Papa. I want my legacy. I want to be in control of my own lands and I want to forge alliances with neighbors. You are content to remain here as Ramsey's general but I am not. Papa, I want my own lands and my own life. If you do not want to return to Blackbog, let me do it. Let me go there and claim the legacy I will inherit from you. Let me be the one to keep the Forbes name in the highlands as something proud and strong."

Jackston was actually take aback at the passionate speech. In truth, it gave him an entirely new perspective seeing it from Donnan's view point, something he hadn't considered before.

"Is that what ye truly feel?" he asked. "Why did ye not say this earlier when we spoke of it?"

Donnan shrugged, looking at the little sister in his arms. She was poking at his nose. "I suppose I had to think on it," he said. "If I stay here, I will never be anything other than your knight. I want to be something more."

It hurt Jackston to hear that but in the same breath, he completely understood it. He didn't want to remain in Scotland because he felt a pull to England. Now, Donnan was feeling the highland blood flowing through his veins and he wanted to answer the call. It was a reversal of roles that Jackston had never really considered.

"Do ye feel as if ye'll be nothin' if ye stay here?" he asked. "If that is the case, I'll send ye back tae de Lohr. He is a man with many properties and...."

Donnan cut him off. "Nay, Papa," he said, "for anywhere de Lohr put me, it would always be at a de Lohr property. Never something all my own. Give me Blackbog, Papa. Give it to me and I swear I shall make you proud."

Jackston was feeling a stab to his heart for reasons he couldn't completely comprehend. All he knew was that his son wanted to leave him. His son wasn't happy to be in his shadow. But as he thought on that, well did Jackston understand that view. No son wanted to be in the shadow of his father. Donnan wanted to forge a new life for himself.

He wanted his legacy.

"Ye have always made me proud, lad," he said, his voice hoarse with emotion. "Ye must forgive me for not realizing ye felt so strongly about yer Scots legacy."

"I suppose I did not realize it myself until we received the missive from Blackbog."

"Are ye sure this is what ye want?"

"I am certain, Papa."

Jackston didn't want to let him go. He looked at Rora, who was sitting with her sewing in her lap, gazing up at her husband. Jackston was looking for some kind of signal from her, disapproval or approval, but all he saw was trust. Trust and hope. She was leaving the decision up to him, like it or not.

Sighing heavily, Jackston returned his attention to Donnan.

"I suppose every man wants something of his very own," he said quietly. "If ye're sure this is what ye want, then I willna deny ye yer legacy."

Donnan broke out in a grin of relief. "I am glad you understand."

Jackston wouldn't let him get too excited about it. "But ye're a *Sassenach*," he pointed out. "It willna be easy for ye. Even as the grandson of Alexander Forbes, the clans may not embrace ye."

"It is a chance I am willing to take. Mayhap you will go with me to Blackbog Castle and introduce me to those you know. It would make it easier for me. Mayhap they would accept me more easily if you did."

Rora stood up from her chair. "Of course he will go with ye," she said. "Yer da will do all he can tae endear ye tae the clans, as the son of Jackston Forbes. It will not be difficult for them tae accept ye, I know it. Mayhap yer da will even find ye a nice Scots lass tae marry. He can arrange an alliance and ye'll be the proudest son the House of Forbes has ever seen."

Donnan stood up and put his arm around his mother's shoulder, kissing her temple. "Thank you, Mother," he said. "I knew you would understand. I… I feel strongly that I must do this."

Jackston looked at the two of them, knowing he was outnumbered. Whether or not he wanted to lose his eldest was of no issue; Donnan had pleaded his case and as much as Jackston didn't want to let his son out of his sight, that's how much he knew the lad had to go. He began to feel rather grieved about it.

"I suppose I knew this day would come, when ye wanted tae spread yer wings and fly the nest," he said, putting a hand on his boy's cheek. "The House of Forbes could ask for no greater legacy than ye, Donnie. If I went home again, my heart wouldna be in it, but yer heart is already full of love for yer heritage. I understand what it is tae follow yer heart."

No truer words were every spoken.

Two weeks later, on a warm summer's day, Donnan and Jackston left Dunster Castle and headed north to Scotland. They traveled in August and into September, when the weather grew cooler but it was still good to travel in.

Late in September, amongst the fields of heather and the dark and rocky hills, Blackbog Castle finally came into view and Lilliana Forbes, very old and very gray, was there to greet them. When Jackston explained that Donnan had come to take charge of Blackbog Castle, the woman wept with joy. Even if her son had no intention of remaining in the highlands, her strong and proud grandson was home to stay and at a gathering of the clans in November, it was Jackston who stood before Ross, MacKay, Menzies, Sutherland, Munro, and Gunn to introduce the new Laird of Blackbog Castle, Donnan Forbes.

He had six marriage offers within the hour.

The Forbes legacy would live on.

THE END

About Kathryn Le Veque

Medieval Just Got Real.

KATHRYN LE VEQUE is a USA TODAY Bestselling author, an Amazon All-Star author, and a #1 bestselling, award-winning, multi-published author in Medieval Historical Romance and Historical Fiction. She has been featured in the NEW YORK TIMES and on USA TODAY's HEA blog. In March 2015, Kathryn was the featured cover story for the March issue of InD'Tale Magazine, the premier Indie author magazine. She was also a quadruple nominee (a record!) for the prestigious RONE awards for 2015.

Kathryn's Medieval Romance novels have been called 'detailed', 'highly romantic', and 'character-rich'. She crafts great adventures of love, battles, passion, and romance in the High Middle Ages. More than that, she writes for both women AND men – an unusual crossover for a romance author – and Kathryn has many male readers who enjoy her stories because of the male perspective, the action, and the adventure.

On October 29, 2015, Amazon launched Kathryn's Kindle Worlds Fan Fiction site WORLD OF DE WOLFE PACK. Please visit Kindle Worlds for Kathryn Le Veque's World of de Wolfe Pack and find many action-packed adventures written by some of the top authors in their genre using Kathryn's characters from the de Wolfe Pack series. As Kindle World's FIRST

Historical Romance fan fiction world, Kathryn Le Veque's World of de Wolfe Pack will contain all of the great story-telling you have come to expect.

Kathryn loves to hear from her readers. Please find Kathryn on Facebook at Kathryn Le Veque, Author, or join her on Twitter @kathrynleveque, and don't forget to visit her website and sign up for her blog at www.kathrynleveque.com.

www.ingramcontent.com/pod-product-compliance
Lightning Source LLC
LaVergne TN
LVHW012034071225
827201LV00035B/459